For my wife, Gill, and for my children: Stuart, Stephen, David, Jonathan and Susie. And for my grandchildren: William, Grace, Sophie, Oliver, Loris and Lucile.

I would like to earnestly thank my son, Stuart, for the enormous guidance and patience he has given me over the many months of editing this book. There's no doubt it helped to lift it to a thoroughly professional level.

I would also like to thank my publisher, Katie Isbester, for her enthusiastic support and superb editing skills. My great thanks also go to Oscar Clarke for his distinctive and very effective illustrations throughout the book, Graeme Critchley for his evocative and dramatic cover art and Ginny Wood for producing such a stunning and elegant design: and for her brilliant flip book idea – a touch of genius!

Contents

Alan watched in horror

Chapter One

It came unexpectedly: a blackness that leaped from the sunshine and swallowed the people standing on the pavement. The brick wall behind flew into boiling dust, then a heart-stop of silence. Alan froze. The roar and spray of fire came rushing across the street towards the library. And the screaming, the screaming. Alan screamed "Mum" in a long drawn-out cry as wave upon shock wave flung itself at the library's windows, sucking them in and out as if to get at Alan. But the crosses of sticky brown paper held the glass panes together and protected Alan from the flying claws of shattered glass.

The bomb had been a big one. It had come from the sky without warning, without the cry of the siren.

The terrible noise stopped and the silence pounded in his head, crushing the words he was trying to find to pull himself back together. Then came the smell: an acrid stabbing of torched metal and charred wood.

Alan stared at the rigid white faces around him. He dropped the book he'd been holding and ran, pushing past the grown ups who swirled around him, noisily, jerkily; their mouths opening and shutting, shouting and crying.

He stopped on the steps outside the Brixton library, his feet crunching on glass and debris. The sun still shone, but across the street, a black cloud of smoke and dust lifted up into the blue sky and spread great arms wide across the roof of the red brick Brixton Town Hall like a black cross of death.

"They didn't have a chance," sobbed a woman's voice. "Just waiting for their milk and orange juice from the family clinic. Mums with their kids."

"God knows how many were there when it fell," added a man's voice.

It was like pain. Alan couldn't see any blood. You didn't need to. The air itself hurt. Torn and wounded.

"Alan!"

"Mum!" Then his head was buried into her chest.

"We'd better get off home," she said.

———•———

"I saw that bomb today," Alan told his best friend Tommy as they sat on the low wall outside his friend's house in Hubert Grove.

"We heard the bang from here," answered Tommy.

"It didn't half go off," Alan said, shivering with the memory of the noise of the explosion and how it had tried to get at him.

"Me dad said there were hundreds killed. Did you see any bodies?"

"Nah, I didn't dare look," said Alan, rubbing his face as though the dust still stuck to his skin.

"Yeah, just be bits, that's all," commented Tommy, nodding.

"My mum was supposed to go in the queue for the orange juice and dried milk," said Alan. "But she left me in the library and popped into Brixton market instead."

"Cor!" said Tommy, but didn't say anything more when he saw Alan's face staring at the pavement.

"They're not supposed to do that," he added angrily. "Ruddy cheats!" he yelled, staring up at the sky and shaking his fist. "Wonder if any of the swines are up there now."

Alan stared up with him. "Nah," he decided. "We could hear them here. It's quiet. Not like Brixton."

Tommy sniffed. "Suppose," he agreed, sounding disappointed.

"Mum says we got to go into the shelter tonight," said Alan.

"It's horrible in ours," said Tommy. "I have to share the bunk with me brother and he kicks me in his sleep."

———•———

Although the Anderson shelter had been dug into the back garden months before, Alan, his sister and his mother had only been down it a few times, and only in the early days, back when everyone expected heavy bombing raids. But then they hadn't come. So his mum, like many other parents, decided it was too much disruption to drag the children from their comfortable beds. The Brixton bomb changed all that. His mother told them that as soon as the air raid siren sounded they all had to get into the shelter.

Alan liked sleeping there. It was exciting with its strange, earthy smell, the flicker of tiny candles and the feeling of safety as he snuggled under the rough blankets and listened to the bombs thumping down on other parts of London. He felt they couldn't find him there.

His sister Sarah didn't like it. "It's pooey," she pronounced.

When the air raids had been a lot less noisy than expected, they used to just go downstairs and sit under the staircase in a cupboard while his mum chatted to old Mrs Smith.

She refused to go into the shelter. "I'm not leaving my comfy bed for those bleeding Gerries," she said.

Mrs Smith lived on her own. She had grey, fluffy

hair and her hands were always covered in white flour from all the baking she did. Alan and Sarah used to love the smell of the buns turning brown in the oven, knowing that as soon as they were ready, Mrs Smith would shout up the stairs: "Cooee, Connie, would the kiddies like to try my buns?"

She knew full well that Alan and Sarah would run thumping down the carpeted stairs and into her kitchen.

She did have one son. He was in the Navy.

"I had a letter from your dad this morning," said Mum that night, turning in her chair to call through to the cupboard. "He's stationed up in Scotland.

Says it's very cold and he wishes he were at home."

Alan missed his dad. But he also felt angry about him being away. He didn't need to be as he wasn't a young man like Mrs Smith's son. He could have stayed at home and looked after them all. Before he left, he used to go out at nights to help rescue people whose houses had been blown up.

Mum said Dad had told her that older men like him could go on being in the heavy air rescue without having to join up. But he'd said he wanted to do his bit. Now he was a long, long way away and hardly ever got home. Mum said he worked on a big gun guarding convoys that sailed around the wild coasts of Scotland. But all the German bombers were down here!

"Where's Scotland, Mum?" asked Sarah.

"It's a long way up north. Too far for him to come home on leave at the moment," said Mum.

"Least he's not being bombed up there," said Mrs Smith. "That one in Brixton today was nasty."

Alan heard his mum's voice drop low.

"We were there," she said, bending forward to speak softly.

"Go on!" said Mrs Smith.

"Alan was in the library. It's only just across the road," Mum went on.

Alan strained to listen.

"I left him there to nip into the market. Five minutes later and we could have been in that queue."

Alan felt himself getting cold and he wrapped the blanket tighter about him, pressing his face into the pillow.

Mrs Smith sighed. "You know, they didn't do that in the last one. Kill ordinary people, women and kids and that. Why'd they do such a thing?"

"I dunno. Mr Thomson in the paper shop says Hitler's trying to scare us into surrendering."

"Flamin' cowards," snorted Mrs Smith. "They ought to do proper fighting with our soldier lads."

"How's your Donald?" asked Mum.

"Fed up," said Mrs Smith. "Freezin' 'is brass monkeys off on those convoys to Russia."

"Must be dangerous with all those U-boats," said Mum.

"See! Even sneaky there. Creeping up on poor unarmed cargo boats and blowing them out of the water," huffed Mrs Smith.

Then the siren came. The slow whine from the bottom of the belly rising to a scream of warning that rippled in waves over the darkened streets.

Alan and Sarah grabbed their blankets and their gas mask boxes and crawled out from the cupboard. Their mum shook the matchbox to make sure there were some left inside.

"You coming, Mrs Smith?" she asked, knowing the answer.

"Them bleeders aren't getting me out of my house," said Mrs Smith. "Go on, get the kiddies down there before they drop one on us."

———•———

It was only a few yards from the back door of Mrs Smith's kitchen to the entrance of the Anderson shelter. Alan looked up. It was quiet after the siren and the sky looked light as if a half moon shone over the black roofs of the houses.

Then, great white bars of light rocketed up into the sky as the searchlights were switched on one by one and they began jiggling backwards and forwards as though playing a game of crossed swords.

Alan and Sarah paused as his mum lit a candle and ducked into the shelter and popped it onto a saucer she left inside on a shelf along one of the corrugated steel walls.

It was like a cave inside. And they were allowed to keep their clothes on when they came here. He and Sarah arranged their blankets onto the wooden bunks, he on the upper one, Sarah below him. The smell of earth was strong, protective, for part of the shelter was dug deep into the ground. It was like a trench with a roof over it. The candlelight waved wobbly shadows along the steel walls like characters from a cartoon.

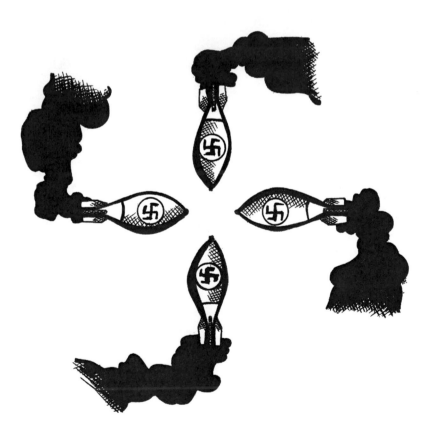

If it's got yer number on it

They felt safe. The steel and the earth could absorb the force of a blast, unless it was a direct hit, although he felt sad leaving the house just waiting there to be bombed. And he worried about Mrs Smith.

"Mum, why doesn't she come here with us?" he asked.

"Says if it's got her number on it, there's nothing she can do to stop it," said his mum.

"What's her number then?" asked Sarah.

"Don't be daft!" sneered Alan.

"Don't shout, there's a love," said Mum. "It means if it's meant to be, it's meant to be."

"Oh," said Sarah, not sure if she really understood.

The first gun banged into the night air. Then another and another, like huge tom-toms warning everyone that the nightly war had started. The ack-ack guns were anchored into the ground of a small park on the other side of the railway. Alan's house was a five-minute walk to a railway stop, which used to be a bonus. Now, Alan wasn't so sure.

Then came the sound that Alan dreaded, the tidal wave of roaring engines as hundreds of German bombers throbbed towards them, looking to find his street, his house, Mrs Smith, his mum, his sister and him.

As the big guns thumped away at the gathering swarm of black bombers, other sounds trickled through; a searing shower of high-pitched whistles that bit into the streets and roads with a crunching remorselessness, and Alan could once again picture the bursting clouds of bricks and plaster and almost taste the blood stinging the screaming air. And this great, throbbing nightmare was creeping closer and closer to him. He rocked on his heels, burying his head into his knees, squeezing his hands tight about his ears. He could hear Sarah crying softly beside him as they both sat on her bunk.

His mother's arms swarmed about his shoulders, crooning: "It's all right, children, they're not coming here, can't you tell, they're moving away now."

Alan lifted his head and listened hard. And, yes, the growling beast was moving away, although he could still hear the deadly whistling of the showers of bombs, and still fear the crashing of explosions. But they weren't coming to bomb Brixton tonight.

Suddenly the curtain hanging across the front door flew open and Timmy, their cat, burst into the shelter followed by next door's tabby.

"Hey look," cried Alan, "Timmy's brought his mate with him!" He and Sarah laughed and their mother, cuddling them both to her chest, laughed too, but with tears in her eyes.

Chapter Two

"Carter?"

"Here, sir."

"Collins?"

"Sir."

"Donaldson?"

"Here, Miss."

Giggles across the classroom. Dopey Donaldson always got confused.

"All right class," said Mr Smiley with a sigh. He was

known as "Smelly" by everyone there, but they liked him. He'd been in the last war and they'd all seen his medals on Remembrance Sunday.

The roll call went on and Alan answered to "Jenkins". But now his heart began to pound and he, like everyone else, was holding his breath as Mr Smiley approached the Ts. Alan glanced quickly across the room to the two empty desks under the window. The Thomas twins sat there. Except today the desks were empty.

"Sorrell?" Mr Smiley paused after reading out the name.

He looked up and into the faces of the children who were staring at him with a strained intensity. He lowered the register to the desk. "I've been told that once… (his voice stumbled but he managed to catch it) that once they're on the mend they'll be coming back to school," he reassured them.

It was just that one wouldn't be able to see again and the other would need a wheelchair. And they didn't have a mother any more; she had been caught in the blast.

Mr Smiley let the noisy outburst of chatter rattle around the room as the children twisted and turned in their seats to talk to each other.

"I thought they'd all been killed," said Tommy to Alan.

"So did I."

"Right class," Mr Smiley called out, and the chattering drifted off into a gentle thunder of boots and shoes rearranging legs under the desk. "We'll send them a card and I'll make sure it gets to their granny, who can take it to the hospital."

Half an hour later, the bell clanged in the hall and the whole class ran screaming and shouting through the door and headed towards the playground. Mr Smiley watched them fly past his desk, his look soft and sad. How many other silences would there be at registration?

Alan and Tommy bashed at each other and

bear-hugged themselves half way to the ground, their voices yelling into each other's ears.

Suddenly a space cleared about them. Alan looked up. Oh no, not Wilkie! The older boy stood there, his face mocking him. Two other boys crowded behind him, jeering.

"Hey Wet Legs, how's yer pants, you peed in them yet?" Wilkie sneered. He was a stocky boy and at ten years old was a class higher than Alan and Tommy.

That ruddy Wilkie never let him forget.

———•———

Wet legs! It all went back to his first day at Stanley Street Infants School four and a half years ago when he was only four. He had been looking forward to going to school. All his mates in the street went there, although Tommy was starting a few months later.

His mum had walked him over the railway bridge and along the two streets to the school gates. It was only when she handed him over to the lady at the entrance and he saw her leaving that he panicked. He began to sniffle.

"Now just stop that, you're not a baby any

more," said the lady gripping him by the arm. As she dragged him down the echoing corridor he tried to look back, but his mum had gone. He sniffed hard and wiped his sleeve over his wet cheeks.

He didn't like this place, he could tell. But the lady was dragging him farther and farther along the corridor and then into a big hall that roared with kids' voices. He tried to hold back, frightened by the shouting and the seething mass of boys and girls.

The lady shoved him amongst some other children his age. "Enid, make sure this one doesn't run away," she ordered a girl in a blue pinafore, who glanced at Alan. "Yes, Miss," she said.

"Don't worry," she whispered to Alan. "We're in Miss Howett's class and she's alright."

"I want my mum," hissed Alan.

Enid caught hold of his hand. "I was just like you on my first day," she sing-songed. "But I got over it. There, there."

Huh! thought Alan to himself. I'm not going to get over it. I'll tell Mum and she'll let me stay at home.

There was a piercing shout, followed by a cracking bang like a huge club striking the wooden floor. Suddenly everyone in the hall went silent. Just like that. The children froze as if in a game.

"Sit!" screamed the voice and everyone fell to the floor in a squatting position. Enid yanked him down beside her.

"It's Miss Perkins, Head of the Infants School," she hissed. "She's a witch, don't look at her!"

Miss Perkins loomed over the assembly and banged her wooden stick and her words marched along with each thump. Alan didn't like her. She *was* like a witch: tight grey bun of hair pulling her face back into a scowl, eyes glinting, her mouth thin and angry. She was glaring at him and he felt a curl of terror slide through him. He felt numb, he couldn't lick his lips, his tongue had dried up and he daren't move his head in case it fell off his shoulders. Then he felt the warm damp spreading inside his trousers.

He held his breath. Could they tell? Could they smell him? He glanced around, but all the kids were staring dumbly to the front.

"Now get up and go to your classes!" the witch finally shrieked and all at once everyone stood up and rushed off to stand in lines to their classrooms.

If he was very careful, he could sneak off before anyone noticed a thing.

"Stand still!" shouted the witch, her eyes glaring at Alan. The children all froze again.

The witch!

"You boy!" Her arm stretched towards the damp patch on the floor at his feet.

"Fetch me the pole!" she ordered.

Another woman walked across to the window and grasped a long wooden pole with a bent hook at one end. She handed it to Miss Perkins. Alan stood trembling from head to toe as the witch raised the pole and lowered the pointed end straight at him.

"This is the boy who has wet himself," she cried. "Look at him! Look at him!" she shrieked.

Alan drained into emptiness. All he could see was the pole and the witch's cruel eyes cursing him.

He never told his mum so she never knew. But Wilkie did. His sister had been in the class and seen what happened and told Wilkie all about it. From that day he'd never let Alan forget the curse of shame that the witch had branded him with.

"Wet legs! You heard!" said Wilkie and grinned at his two followers. "Pees in his pants he does."

They shrieked with glee. "Wets himself!" they yelled and jabbed each other's arms.

Alan stood up and Tommy stood back slightly. Alan felt a dull, cold weight rolling around his belly. Wilkie's finger was poking into his chest and he saw the boy's mouth making ugly shapes.

He was in a cocoon of muffled noises that thumped and banged and the screams of yesterday squeezed his head tighter and tighter. And then it burst. There was a burning in his chest, a flame of pure rage, someone cried out and an arm lurched up and something soft scrunched beneath a fist and in a whirl of madness he crashed into Wilkie and, almost sobbing, flung him to the ground and tried to pound the shouting boy flattened beneath him.

Abruptly, he was hauled to his feet and Miss Foster's voice cracked beside him. "Stop it, stop it! What are you doing to that boy?"

Alan looked down panting and Wilkie was crying and clutching a bleeding nose. His mates dragged him upright. "'E hit me, Miss," Wilkie complained. "He's a madman."

"Go and see Nurse and get cleaned up," ordered Miss. "And you, young Jenkins, what on earth came over you?"

"Wilkie was having a go at him, Miss," said Tommy. Miss looked at them both.

"Alan Jenkins should be reported. I'll have to tell Mr Strong and see what he says," she announced at last. "Now get back to your class."

"I think she's pleased you whacked Wilkie," said Tommy digging a finger into Alan's side. "He certainly didn't expect that."

Nor had Alan. He couldn't understand the rage that had burnt away the fear and the shame. Ever since he had seen those empty desks in the class-room, he'd felt a strange mood trembling through him. It was gone now.

"Ruddy 'eck, he'll kill me next time!" said Alan, suddenly aware of the consequences.

"Doubt it," said Tommy. "I think you terrified him."

The desk lids banged up and down in a slamming battery of noise. "I've seen Sheila's knickers!" cried Arthur Smith, and his shining face mooned over the top of Alan's desk lid. Arthur was always claiming to have seen some girl's knickers; he didn't have a sister and felt left out of things.

Alan ignored him and carried on talking to Tommy. "Look, you sure you haven't seen Wilkie and his gang waiting for me out there."

"Nah," said Tommy. "He only whacks the ones that don't fight back. Look at poor weedy William. Gets bashed every break time – and has to hand over his cold toast."

Cold toast! Alan sighed. The smell of it! Buttery, slightly burnt. He'd asked his mum to pack him up some toast because he was starving by the milk break. But she said it was silly having it cold. Much nicer just warmly crisped and freshly buttered.

Charley Jones and Fred Thomas crashed into Alan's desk, clinging to each other in a grunting, huffing wrestling match as they rolled and fell to the wooden floor trying to get a stranglehold on the other's throat.

"Fight! Fight! Fight!" chanted Arthur Smith but no one bothered to join in, as the two boys were always wrestling each other. They were the best of friends.

"Dunno," said Alan doubtfully, moving his legs out of the way of Charley's kicking feet. "He might feel I've shamed him in front of his mates."

"He won't," Tommy reassured him. "He ain't that tough. And anyway he ain't got no mates."

Monica Simmons screamed a high-pitched yell as Arthur grabbed her long hair, and then he shouted in pain as she grabbed his nose and yanked it hard.

The door opened and Mr "Smelly" walked into the classroom. The desk lids stopped banging. Arthur quickly returned to his desk holding his nose, and Charley and Fred scrambled to their feet and hurried to their places. The class was quiet at last.

Mr Smiley didn't look at them or even seem surprised at the sudden change as the children all sat up straight and waited for him to speak. He very rarely ever shouted, unlike most of the other teachers.

"Right, Tommy. You're ink monitor and don't spill it or we'll be back on the slates again."

Alan hated the slates. Trying to scratch letters onto them took forever. And they never looked right.

Tommy walked around the desks carefully tipping the sharp-smelling black ink jug into the tiny inkwells.

"Spelling," announced Mr Smiley. The class groaned as he walked to the blackboard and began writing out a list of words in chalk.

"Remember, spelling is the secret of words, and words are the secret of your life's story."

His voice trailed off into some sort of dreamy fantasy. Alan had once overheard him telling another teacher that he hoped he could light a spark in one of the kids and send him out into the world with a good chance of making it and doing something special. The other teacher had simply shaken his head. "They're only cannon fodder," he'd replied, and Alan wondered what that meant.

Alan dipped his pen in the ink, bent down low over the sheet of lined paper on his desk and started to copy the words out in block capitals, his tongue licking his lips in concentration. He was supposed to do joined-up writing at his age but none of the teachers seemed to care what he did, or how well he did, as long as he kept quiet and didn't bother them.

"Just to warn you," said Mr Smiley after a few minutes, "some of the words aren't spelled correctly."

"Oh no," said Alan. "That's not fair!" Smelly was the only one who seemed to try to teach them anything, worse luck.

He looked at the list he had copied out and sighed.

And then the sirens whined out their warning and saved them all. "Right, pens down and line up, no pushing or shoving and follow me to the shelter," said Mr Smiley.

———•———

They sat on long benches in the school cellars, which were used as an air raid shelter. The noise was deafening as every kid down there shouted and screamed to their friends. The teachers ignored them for once, gathering inside an office at one end of the long, vaulted room and drinking cups of tea from an enamel urn. Alan kept glancing around him to make sure there was no sign of Wilkie and his mates.

"Let's bunk off," shouted Tommy above the din.

"I dunno," said Alan, thinking he was in enough trouble already. He still hadn't been summoned to see the headmaster about hitting Wilkie.

"Go on, we're in old Miss Richards' class next, and she never knows who's there or not," urged Tommy. Given that Miss Richards was as deaf as a post and could barely see through her old wire-framed glasses, it was hardly surprising she had no idea who was missing from her class.

"Oh, all right then," Alan said.

"Yeah, soon as the all-clear's sounded," said Tommy.

The ack-ack guns boomed from the nearby park, slightly muffled by the thick walls of the cellar, and occasionally dust sifted down from the old brickwork. It made you cough a bit. Alan wondered if the cellar would stand up to a direct hit but supposed that the old class buildings built above the cellar would take most of the explosion. They were probably safer there than in their Anderson shelter in the back garden. Alan couldn't hear any bombers droning overhead and for the first time that day, he relaxed.

Chapter Three

It was dead easy to slip away from school. When the all-clear sounded, the kids rushed up the steps and out into the playground, milling about all over the place as the teachers tried to get them into class lines.

Alan and Tommy just slipped through the crowd and out of the side gate and into the street outside.

It was quiet after the noisy playground. No one was about and they felt like they could go and do whatever they wanted, and no one would be bothered. A far-away fire engine bell clanged and there was a pall of black smoke drifting high into the blue sky a long way off over the Clapham skyline.

"Where we going then?" asked Alan.

"Let's go and look at the guns," suggested Tommy.

"Yeah!" They skipped and hollered their way down the empty street and around the corner to the small park where the big ack-ack guns had been dug in.

They stared through the iron railings. The long slender snouts of the guns were steaming slightly.

"Do you reckon they shot any Gerries down?" wondered Tommy.

"Dunno. What happens then?" asked Alan. "I mean, do they always blow the bombers to smithereens or... do they come down in flames and crash into houses?"

Tommy looked at Alan, perplexed. "S'funny, I always thought they'd blow up in the sky. Must be heavy things. Wouldn't fancy something like that landing on me 'ead."

"Where's Jumbo?" Alan asked suddenly. Tommy stared upwards, but there was no sign of the great silk balloon that normally swayed high above the park like a fat but graceful elephant.

"It's over there," he announced, and pointed to it lying on the ground, deflated, grey and shrivelled.

"Shouldn't you two be at school?" a man's voice asked suddenly.

A soldier stood there, wearing a tin helmet and armed with a rifle, on the other side of the railings.

"Been sent home – broken windows," Tommy told him.

"Likely story," the soldier sniffed. "Just remember there's live ammo here and you don't want to be messing about."

"No mister," said Tommy. "Come on Alan." And the two boys wandered off to the old almshouses.

They were abandoned now as they overlooked the gun park. The doors and windows were boarded up but, here and there, planks had been ripped aside where kids had broken in to explore.

"You been in there?" asked Tommy.

"Nah, it's only where smelly old people used to live," said Alan, though he had no memory of the people who had once called the place their home.

"Me gran lived there and she weren't smelly," Tommy protested.

"Oh," said Alan. And then thought of Mrs Smith in the downstairs flat at home. She was pretty old and she didn't smell either.

Just then, a door burst open behind them and someone came whirling past. "Run! Run! Run!" he yelled as he flew up the street his arms windmilling in panic. He looked vaguely familiar but they hadn't seen his face. They sprinted after him, too frightened to look behind, just in case. They kept running for a few hundred yards till the boy in front staggered to a halt and leaned against a brick wall, chest heaving, bent over and gasping hoarsely. They pulled up and leaned down, resting their hands on their legs and sucking in great breaths.

"Why," began Alan. Cough, wheeze. "Why we running?" He managed to squeeze out the words.

The boy turned. It was Wilkie! "Ruddy soldier

with a great big gun trying to kill me," he gasped. "'S you!" he added, surprised.

"Why was he trying to kill you?" Tommy asked, turning around to make sure that there was no one with a gun chasing them.

"Nicked his satchel," explained Wilkie. "But I had to chuck it quick when he nobbled me. You scarpered from school?"

"Yeah," said Tommy. "It was only Miss Richards' class next."

"Daft bat. I bunk off most of the classes. 'Cept Mr Carroll's. He gives you a right battering if he catches you," said Wilkie. "Fancy a fag?" he added, pulling out a green paper packet of Woodbines.

"Yeah," said Alan. Tommy nodded dubiously. The last time his dad had been home on leave, Alan had nicked some of his Army issue fags. He hadn't much liked smoking but when Wilkie produced a box of matches, Alan leaned over to light his fag from the lit match cupped in his hand, the smoke drifting over his face, reminding him of his dad lighting a fag in the kitchen when he was home on leave. Tommy copied him.

Wilkie leaned back, took a deep drag and blew out a large puff of cigarette smoke. "That's better," he said with a satisfied sigh. "Nothing like a ciggie to steady yer nerves when you've had a brush with death."

Alan shook his head, struggling to stop the smoke from exploding in his lungs. Tommy burst out coughing and spluttering.

"Can't take it like us big boys, can he?" Wilkie said, grinning at Alan who felt a warm glow; his worst enemy had suddenly become his best mate.

"I'm off down the bombsite to meet the gang. Fancy coming?" said Wilkie, stubbing out his fag on the sole of his boot, then blowing on the end of it before stuffing it back into the cigarette packet.

The bombsite, which was not far from the Clapham North tube station at the end of Alan's road, had once been a square of houses that had been blown up and burnt to the ground early on in the Blitz. It was now a dumping ground for anything dragged out from other bombed houses that scavengers decided was of no value. In the centre was an old burnt-out car and nearby someone had lit a fire from scraps of wood. There were about half a dozen boys of different ages standing around the fire, while a couple of them sat in old armchairs, their stuffing bursting through the torn fabric.

"Wotcher, Wilkie," one of the boys called out. "Tosher," nodded Wilkie. "Me mates, Alan and Tommy," he added by way of introduction. Tosher was a freckled, flame-haired lad with a raw face that looked as if it was always on the look out for a fight. He glanced at the two newcomers and nodded.

"Got no mum or dad," said Wilkie. "Blown up."

Alan and Tommy stared at the orphan who was poking at a raw potato lying at the edge of the fire.

"Supposed to live with his gran, but he's bunked down in an empty house in Cottage Grove," said Wilkie.

Duggie, Leader of the Gang

Alan knew Cottage Grove. Half its houses were abandoned and the rest were occupied by adults who hardly came out but stared through windows half covered by dirty curtains, their kids sitting on the pavement with grubby faces and torn clothes. The clinging smell of boiled cabbages always made Alan feel sick. He knew the families were poor, far poorer than his own family. They never seemed to have any work. 'Keep away from there,' his mum had warned him but never explained why.

"Got any fags?" A big fifteen-year-old lad joined them. Dirty-faced with blond, lank hair and long, shabby trousers, he stood there waiting. His eyes stared demandingly, steady and cold. Alan glanced away, not wanting to catch his attention.

Wilkie hurriedly dragged the packet out of his trouser pocket and thrust it at the boy. "Sure, Duggie, help yourself."

"Ta mate. See yer," said Duggie when Wilkie had lit him up and the big boy went back to a group of older boys on the other side of the fire.

"Been in the nick, he has," said Wilkie proudly.

"What for?" asked Tommy.

"Bust his dad's nose and whacked a copper," explained Wilkie. "Don't argue with him," he added, unnecessarily, thought Alan, as he watched Duggie slowly walk with the splayed out feet of someone who knew he didn't have to worry about anyone around here. He was king.

"He still at school?" asked Tommy.

Wilkie snorted. "Duggie?! They couldn't keep him in. Nah, he runs his own gang, like."

"How d' yer mean?" asked Tommy.

"These lot. Others like," said Wilkie. "Sort of organises them."

Alan looked over to where Duggie was talking softly to the group by the fire. All the boys listened intently.

"Anyfink you need, he'll get it for you," said Wilkie.

"Wot, nicking stuff?" asked Tommy.

"Mostly lying about," said Wilkie. "There's a lot after a raid."

"Isn't that looting?" Alan asked.

Wilkie snorted. "Only if you get caught. Find all sorts: radios, gramophones, furniture. Duggie can get a price for anything. Through contacts," he added, tapping the side of his nose.

"What, crooks?" asked Alan.

"Don't ask," warned Wilkie.

Alan felt a shudder, as though someone had opened a door and a threatening chill had wafted out from a place where something dark lurked.

"Let's get back," he said. "It's dinner time and there's semolina pudding today. You coming?" he asked the others.

Tommy nodded.

"Nah, I'll stay here and see what's up," said Wilkie.

When Alan looked back, Wilkie had joined the gang. Duggie had put his arm around his shoulders and was talking to the other boys.

Chapter Four

Alan and Tommy lay stretched out along the top girder of the footbridge that arched over from their street, spanning the South Coast railway line. The studded metal lay warm beneath their bellies and the sun tickled their backs. It was their favourite lookout spot.

Beneath them, the bright railway tracks streaked away in both directions. Alan thought of it as a river. In one direction, it flowed in silver lines towards

Dreaming of trains

the centre of London: Big Ben, Trafalgar Square, the King in his palace, and old Churchill deep in his bunker, fat cigar plugged between his lips, growling out orders to his Air Force, his battleships and his soldiers waiting in their thousands, ready to fight the Germans if they dared to invade. Alan wondered if his dad got orders from Mr Churchill, telling him to keep his eyes peeled sharp just in case the Nazis tried to sneak in through Scotland.

On the opposite side, the lines streamed into the countryside, leaping across fields and farms until they reached the edge of the land where the sea churned and rushed beneath the barbed wire to hiss high onto the sandy beach. Beyond the waves, who knew what waited to pounce out of the mists?

Alan wanted to live in a house beside the railway tracks. It would be like living on the banks of a river. He loved the roaring sound of the trains whooshing past, the smoke blanketing out the world. Both Wilkie and Tommy lived in houses on the banks of the railroads.

Neither he nor Tommy had ever been inside Wilkie's house. They didn't really want to in any case. Standing on the doorstep you caught the sharp stink of stale food and sweat. Alan's kitchen had a warm whiff of egg and chips. And Tommy's mum was always baking cakes. Not that Wilkie ever invited them inside. He always closed the door quickly behind him to stop them from seeing anything.

Wilkie's dad was a frightening man. He was short but strong, with eyes that glared at everyone. Tommy reckoned he beat Wilkie a lot. And Wilkie always jumped whenever his dad called him. He never shouted but it was a voice that made you hope he never called your name.

"That bloke Duggie's scary," said Tommy.

"Wilkie reckons a lot about him," Alan replied.

"Dodgy getting involved though," said Tommy.

"Guess Wilkie wants to be in his gang," added Alan. Tommy hissed with misgiving.

They both stared down the tracks.

"Our Jack's done a runner," said Tommy.

"Oh yeah, back home is he?" asked Alan.

"Yeah, turned up last night."

Tommy's brother was in the Army, or was supposed to be.

"He's not a coward or anyfink. But he hates being up in Yorkshire. Says he can't understand a bleedin' word they say. So he's come back to civilisation. That's what he told me dad," explained Tommy.

"Won't they be looking for him here?" Alan wondered aloud.

"He's gone up in the attic," said Tommy. "Then he and Gloria are going to me gran's in Stockwell." Gloria was Jack's sweetheart.

"Train coming!" yelled Tommy, and they both leaned over the edge and stuck their heads out waiting for the steam locomotive to burst out beneath them.

The grey and black smoke boiled up from below and swallowed their heads in a billowing cloud of coal dust, grease and steam.

"Whee!!" They whooped together and laughed as they looked at each other's sooty faces.

Below, the big flat trucks pounded rhythmically along the line, carrying tanks and armoured cars. They stared in fascination at the gun barrels pointing towards them.

"Pah! Pah!" Tommy shouted aiming his finger at them. "Drrrr!" Alan rattled, mowing down the Gerries scrambling to man the guns.

"There's too many of them," yelled Tommy. "Quick, before they find our range," and with that he slid off the girder and leaped to the ground.

They ran down the steps of the footbridge three at a time and raced around the corner and into their street. They pulled up suddenly at the sight of an army jeep parked by the kerb. A military policeman stood beside it.

"They're in your house," said Alan.

"Yeah, must be after Jack," said Tommy.

"He's armed," said Alan, nodding towards the MP by the jeep. He had a holstered pistol jammed into his white belt. "They ain't gonna shoot him are they?"

For an answer, Tommy looked desperately around himself, then picked up half a brick lying in the gutter. "They better not," he said, his face squeezed with anger and fear.

Alan grabbed his arm. "Don't Tommy, they might shoot you."

Then the door of Tommy's house burst open and a fight spilled out on to the steps leading up to it. Two MPs were trying to wrap their arms around a tall, burly figure who was yelling and swearing as he tried to get his punches in.

"They've got your Jack."

The three men stumbled down the steps. One of the MPs got an armlock around Tommy's brother, while his colleague tried to handcuff his wrists. Another MP raced over and pinned Jack against the low wall in front of the house. Jack kneed him in the groin and the policeman sank to his knees.

"Get him, Jack!" shouted Tommy.

But the other two had caught both of his brother's arms and soon had his wrists locked behind his back. "Gotcher!" they yelled.

"Get off him!" cried Tommy, and Alan gripped him even harder and made him drop the half-brick.

Jack was grabbed by his short hair and dragged towards the jeep, while one of the policemen thumped him hard in the back.

Just before he was thrown into the rear seat of the jeep, Jack twisted his head around, his face red and bruised. He grinned at the boys, and a trickle of blood slid from the side of his mouth.

"See ya, Tommy!" he shouted. "See ya, Alan!"

"See ya, Jack," said Tommy and Alan together and waved as the vehicle sped off. There was still a scrap of sorts going on in the back seat.

"That your Jack getting nicked?" asked a voice behind them. It was Wilkie.

"Yeah, rotten devils," answered Tommy with feeling.

"Never guess what?" Wilkie went on, "I'm in. Big Duggie's gang. Says I can be part of his wassisname."

"Wassisname?" asked Alan.

"Nah, not just that. His, his... organisation," Wilkie drew out the last word with wonder, and jabbed his finger at his chest. "Make some dosh, eh? Whajer fink?"

"I fink you're nuts," said Alan.

"Nah, I've got you two in it as well," said Wilkie. "We can be a right team, us three."

"Not on your nelly," said Alan.

"It'll be all right," reassured Wilkie. "Nuffin dodgy... just clearing up is all."

"Looting," corrected Alan. "You can get shot for that."

"Yer what!" exclaimed Tommy.

"He's talking stupid," said Wilkie. "It ain't like that at all. Duggie told me. Stuff we find has been left behind. No one wants it, it's like we're doing everyone a favour."

"How d'yer know no one wants it?" asked Tommy.

"Well..." replied Wilkie, "they're either gone away to be re-housed or they're sort of dead."

"I can't believe you!" said Alan.

"Look, 's all right, you just have to help me get the stuff back to Duggie, I'll do the searching and finding. Be money in it for you."

"Count me out," said Alan.

"Me too," said Tommy.

"Well," began Wilkie, looking awkward, "Can't, see. 'Cos I promised Duggie you'd be in, and if you wasn't like ...it could go nasty for me."

"How d' you mean?" asked Tommy.

"He said if I ratted on him, I'd end up in a bomb crater with a ton of bricks on me head," confessed Wilkie.

"You idiot!" said Alan and began to walk away.

"Honest, it's nothing illegal," cried Wilkie.

Tommy ran up to walk beside Alan.

"What we gonna do, Al?" asked Tommy. "Can't just let Duggie... you know."

"Gawd knows," replied Alan.

Chapter Five

You could always tell when a tube train was coming. Like dragon's breath, hot air blew out of the deep, dark throat of the tunnel, billowing stale dust and old newspapers. Then the tracks began to whisper thinly, threateningly, like a snake slithering into the attack. Alan stared at the middle track where the electric current ran and couldn't help but edge back against his mum.

It was as if he could hear it sizzling with electric

fire. He hated the Clapham North tube station because lines ran on both sides of the one central platform.

It was like standing on the deck of a ship; tidal waves of screaming trains smashing past on either side made him feel wobbly, as though he were in danger of being sucked overboard.

A gradual grumble of noise built up inside the tunnel, booming, louder and louder, until the red train burst out of the darkness with a crashing of metal wagons, screaming wheels and flying air that charged down the side of the platform, finally stopping with a huge hiss of brakes. It then stood there, engines throbbing. Its electric doors sighed open and banged against their stoppers. Alan slowly let his breath out, glad that he, once again, hadn't fallen onto the electric line.

He was off with his mum and his sister, Sarah, to see their Aunty Vi in King's Cross. It took them an hour to get there. His aunt was lucky. She lived in a flat above the mainline railway tracks running into the huge terminus, and Alan spent hours watching the trains shuffling and rattling across the webs of railway lines, breathing in the warm smoke of the coal-fired locomotives puffing up into the air.

"You hear from Jim lately?" his mum asked Aunty Vi.

"Got a letter last month. Took six weeks to get here, though."

Uncle Jim was a prisoner of war in Germany. He had been captured during the retreat to Calais a year earlier. His truck had run out of petrol on the outskirts of the port and his unit had been rounded up by the German army.

"How's he getting on?"

"He says they're managing, though the Red Cross parcels are few and far between. Thinks the Gerry guards are nicking them," said Aunty Vi. "Been having to boil up potato peelings to fill up."

"He'll be skin and bones then," said Mum. "He

was thin enough before he left."

"Why don't he dig a tunnel and escape, Aunty?" asked Alan.

His aunt and mum chuckled.

"I don't think your Uncle Jim's the hero type, bless him," said his aunt. "Apart from which, he doesn't sound as if he's got the strength to do any digging. I could never get him to do any gardening when he was here, Connie, could I?" and she and Mum burst into loud laughter. "No, I just want the old bugger to survive and come on back home to me," said his aunt, her voice going funny.

Alan's mum put her arms around her and gave her a squeeze. "He'll be all right, just you see."

His aunt sniffed and stood up. "Course he will," she said. "Now, come on you two kids, let's have some jam tarts. I made them especially for you."

———•———

It was getting dark when they left Aunty Vi's house and the streets were quiet, with not many taxis or buses about.

They went down the long, white-tiled corridors that led to the lower platforms at Kings Cross tube station, a much grander affair than Clapham North. This looked like a proper station, with a big ticket office. A lot of trains left from here on different lines, not just the Northern Line, but also the Circle, the Victoria, the Metropolitan, and the Piccadilly. Alan studied the long lists of stations and didn't recognise half of them. Some looked like they were a long way out into the countryside like

Chorleywood, Dollis Hill and Arnos Grove – full of birdsong and rustling trees. He wished they could catch a train there, away from the bombs, the air raid shelters… and gangs like the one that Duggie ran. He worried that somehow Wilkie would get him involved.

Their train stopped at Elephant and Castle. The engine hummed and then suddenly died. A voice began echoing along the platform.

"Everybody out, please, everybody out."

"What's going on, Mum?" asked his little sister, Sarah.

"I dunno, love, but this train's not going any-where so let's ask when the next one is coming along," replied Mum.

On the platform, people were milling about looking angry and confused, waving their arms at a middle-aged platform guard who was pointing down the tracks and shrugging his shoulders.

Alan's mother joined the crowd.

"Excuse me, but how long do we have to wait for the next train? We've got to get to Clapham North," she asked the station attendant.

"You'll have to wait till six tomorrow morning, missus," he said. "Big bomb's hit a power station along the route and it will take all night to fix it."

"But," protested their mother, "I've got two

children with me. What are we supposed to do?"

"Don't worry, missus, you'll do what hundreds round here do every night – sleep on the platform."

"But we haven't got anything for bedding."

"That's all right, there's a lady be along soon with some blankets and pillows."

"Cor!" said Alan to his sister. "Hear that? We're sleeping here all night."

Sarah pulled a face. "I don't want to lie on some dirty old platform. I want my bed. Mum!"

"Sorry Sarah, we'll just have to do the best we can till the morning."

As the night drew on, more and more people

began to arrive on the platform carrying bedding and baskets of food. They all seemed to know one another.

"If I was you, duck," said a big, fat elderly woman to Alan's mum, "I should grab a spot for you and your kiddies before they're all used up."

They found a spot close to the entrance to the tunnel and a rather bossy woman arrived and spoke to their mum. "Could I have your name and address please. We like to keep track of the people here. And then I can issue you all with the requisite bedding."

"She's a posh one," whispered Alan to Sarah. But at least they got their blankets and pillows.

"I wouldn't like to sleep near the tunnel," said a boy's voice. Alan looked around, and saw a boy his own age, dressed in grey short trousers and a grubby jumper, standing there. "Yeah, you hear funny noises in the night, coming from down there."

"Oh yeah," said Alan.

"Me gran says it's all the ghosts of people killed in the Blitz. They don't know they're dead and they're trying to find their way home," said the boy.

"Gerroff," said Alan, but stared down into the black depths of the tunnel. When he turned around the boy had gone.

While his mum made up their beds, Alan decided

to stroll along the platform, carefully stepping over legs and feet. They all seemed to know each other, laughing and gossiping and swapping books and newspapers. Someone was playing an accordion and a short, tubby woman was jigging her legs up and down to the music, showing her stocking tops.

Alan wandered off the platform through one of the short exits that led to the stairs and then on to the big escalators that took passengers up to the streets. He saw a chocolate machine fixed to a wall and stared at it longingly. Inside were the distinctive mauve packets of Cadbury's chocolate bars. But Alan knew they were just pretend, because he and

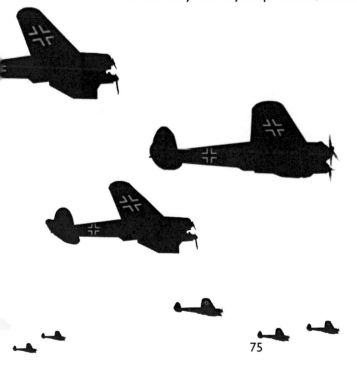

The ghosts don't know they're dead

Tommy had once managed to prise one open and discovered they were made of cardboard inside the alluring shiny covers.

He turned the corner and saw a group of men huddled together. One of them had an Army kitbag and the other two were handing him money. The one with the kitbag jerked his head this way and that, saw Alan, winked, and then reached into the bag, pulled out a number of packets and handed them over. The two men stuffed them inside their jackets and hurried away.

"Yer mum want any fags, butter or cheese, sonny?" the man called out to Alan.

"I dunno."

"Well, I'm here every night if she does. Got nylons an' all," the man added and then settled back against the wall to wait for the next customer.

"Where've you been? You shouldn't wander off like that," his mum scolded Alan when he returned. "What have you been up to?" she asked when she saw his face.

"Nuffin. Honest," said Alan. "Just been looking around, that's all."

"Like a cup of tea, dearie?" It was the fat woman who had spoken to them earlier. She had a thermos flask in one hand and a tin mug in the other.

"Oh, that would be lovely," said Alan's mum. "Are you here every night then?"

"Bless you, it's safer down here than anywhere," said the woman. "Name's Gertie."

"Connie," replied Alan's mum. "Not very comfortable though, is it?"

Gertie poured out the tea already with milk in it and handed it over. "Oh, we all bring our own pillows and that, and it's a nice crowd down here. And we're left alone."

Alan thought of the spiv. "There's a man who says he's got cheese and butter and things down there," he told his mum.

"Oh you mean Crafty Charlie," laughed Gertie. "He gets all sorts. Black market like. His prices ain't bad, though. But don't touch his nylons, they ladder as soon as you look at them. My neighbour Flo bought a big box of chocolates as a present for her mum and when she opened them, they were all just dried bits of tar. Knew the bloke's ma an' all." She tutted and shook her head. "Who can yer

trust if you can't trust yer own kind?"

Alan's mum shook her head sadly. "Too true," she murmured.

"Anyway, I'm off for me stout and me kip. See yer in the morning. 'Night." And Gertie walked off.

The station lights were dimmer now. Alan listened hard. A soft moaning sound swirled deep down inside the black tunnel. He shivered and pulled the rough blanket over his head and snuggled against his mum. It was going to be a long night.

Chapter Six

It was Saturday morning, so Alan and Tommy were sitting outside Tommy's house on the low wall. Once there had been iron railings all along it but they had been hacked off and taken away for the war effort.

"Lot o' good that old scrap iron'll be," commented Tommy's dad. "Might make a few arrow heads and that's about it."

"Did you hear any ghosts?" Tommy wanted to

know, after Alan told him about sleeping on the tube platform.

"No, but there was some funny noises going on in the tunnel. You don't know what's down there". Tommy shivered. "We didn't half have to get up early. The train came in at half past five and they made us get up and get on it." Alan yawned loudly and stretched his arms.

"Look out, there's Wilkie," said Tommy. But he'd already spotted them so they couldn't sneak off.

"Hey, you two!" Wilkie called out. "Got any fags, only me dad's nicked mine, the bleeder."

"Sorry Wilkie, me mum don't smoke and me dad's away," said Alan. Tommy just shook his head and Wilkie shrugged his shoulders and sat down beside them.

"Fancy going down the bombsite?" he asked.

Alan looked down at the ground. "Dunno, me mum says I gotta be in for dinner early."

"Don't be a soft twerp," scoffed Wilkie. "Anyway, there's plenty of time."

"Look," Alan burst out, "I don't want to get involved with that bloke, Duggie."

Wilkie laughed, but it wasn't a very convincing one. "You don't have to. 'S only me he wants and anyway he won't be down there today. That's just one of his places. He has kids all over …collecting for him."

Tommy snorted but said nothing.

"Nah, but come on. It's boring round here," urged Wilkie.

Tommy and Alan looked at each other, and then stood up.

"Great," said Wilkie.

———•———

There weren't many at the bombsite, just a few young boys playing gangsters in and around the wrecked car.

"What sort of car is that?" asked Tommy as he sat down beside the other two on the old sofa.

"Morris 8," said Wilkie with certainty. "Belonged to an old couple who lived here before it was bombed. Tight lot, stuck up and that 'cos they were the only ones in the street who had a car. Never spoke to no one. Serves 'em right," he added, pointing his chin at what was left of the car.

Tommy looked at the gang of kids scrambling in and around it.

"Don't mind them," said Wilkie. "Hey, you lot, get off out of there," he yelled.

"Get off yerself," said one of them, a scrawny boy, with a blotchy red face and a runny nose.

Wilkie got up and walked over to the car. The boy glared at him defiantly. Wilkie casually whacked him around the head and sent him flying to the ground. "Do as yer told."

The boy got to his feet, yelling and crying at the same time. "I'll get me big bruvver onto you. He's in the commandos and he can kill with his bare hands."

"Yeah! Him and who's army? Now scarper," said Wilkie, climbing into the driver's seat of the car.

Tommy and Alan climbed over the broken doors and into the front seat beside him. Wilkie pretended to rev up the engine. "Brrrm! Brrrrm!!" He spun the steering wheel and made skidding noises.

"Have to watch it on the bends," he warned. "Suspension's a bit knackered."

"Yeah," agreed Tommy, solemnly. He had never been in a car before.

"Where shall we go?" asked Wilkie.

"Let's go to the seaside," cried Alan.

"Yeah!" said Tommy, who had never been to the seaside in his life.

"Right then, hang on to yer hats," said Wilkie,

and with that he wiggled the gear stick jutting up from the floor. "Whoom!" he shouted. "We'll be there in a flash."

———•———

Later, the boys strolled down into the back streets of Brixton, on to Stockwell Road and past the Odeon cinema. They gazed at a black-and-white poster advertising a western. "Roy Rogers, yeah!" said Wilkie, fast-drawing his finger out of his torn pocket. "Blah! Blah! Blah!"

"Ahhh!" yelled Tommy and rolled onto the pavement. "He got me, Alan," he cried and stiffened into a corpse.

"Trigger," sighed Alan, looking at the poster of the cowboy on the horse. "You ever ride a horse, Wilkie?"

"Sat on Dusty John's old nag once," said Wilkie.

"'S not the same," said Alan. Dusty John was the local rag-and-bone man. He went round the streets with his horse and cart, collecting any old stuff that people wanted to throw away.

"Yeah, he never moved even though I yelled at him," said Wilkie. "He was all bones anyway."

"I rode a donkey once at a fair on Clapham

Common," said Tommy, getting up from the pavement and dusting down his trousers.

"Mum says she'll take me to the flicks when Dad's allowance comes through," said Alan, jerking his chin at the poster.

"Don't pay to go in, do yer?" said Wilkie, shocked. "Bunk in through the back. I always do."

"Yee how!" yelled Tommy, and rode his horse away at a gallop, urging it on down the street with a whack on his hips.

"He's getting away," cried Alan and he and Wilkie slapped their sides as they took off after the baddie.

They hauled themselves in at the corner, puffing

and panting. "There's an old sweet factory down there," said Wilkie. "Got blown up by a big bomb. Anything left, the incendiaries took care of. Reckon there's any sweets left behind?"

Alan licked his mouth. Sweets! He couldn't remember what they tasted like.

"We could look," said Tommy.

"Come on then," and they trotted down the narrow street and around the corner where their feet crunched across broken glass and pulverised bricks.

The factory was a tall building, its roof gone and its walls licked by great black scorch marks where the flames had tried to devour its sides. Its windows had all been blown out, leaving only tattered wooden frames leaning at crazy angles within the openings. It didn't smell like a sweet factory, just stale ash and dirty water.

"Well, it used to make sweets before the war. Let's go and explore," said Wilkie. They found one of the corrugated tin panels loose in what had once been a side entrance into the works. More glass crunched under their boots and the smell of old burnt rubber almost made them choke. Cable wires hung down like jungle creepers from the steel beams above them.

"Over here!" yelled Wilkie.

They shoved their way around some old tin drums that were filled with blackened ash and stepped carefully through a heavy metal door hanging on its hinges. A pane of glass slid heavily to the floor with a crash that made them jump. They were inside some kind of storehouse; papers and tins were spread across the floor in a sodden mash of rubbish. A huge, badly-scorched cupboard leaned at an angle over a massive porcelain sink.

"Wonder what's in here," said Wilkie and pulled its door wide open. A metallic stream of mugs clattered down upon him, followed by the clunk of a large brown steel kettle, which narrowly missed

his head. "Ow! Ow! Ow!" he cried as the mugs bounced off him.

"Over here," cried Tommy. "There's some stairs going up."

Sure enough, a broad stone staircase rose above the floor through an archway. As they climbed, the steps narrowed until eventually they turned into a twisting wrought-iron ladder. They reached another metal door, pushed it open and a rush of cool air flowed in. Tommy scrambled up the ladder. "Wow," he said, "we're on the roof."

Alan followed the others onto what was left of the rooftop, which wasn't much. In front of them stretched a wide girder and beside it ran a stone parapet.

"There's nothing up here," he said. "Let's go back and find another way." He didn't fancy staying up here. He looked up at the sky. It was empty of planes. Still, it was too exposed.

"Nah," said Wilkie. "We can cross over here and see what's on the other side." And he stepped confidently onto the parapet and began to stride along the narrow wall. Tommy followed him.

Alan took a deep breath and climbed gingerly onto the parapet. His chest hurt because his heart was thumping hard against his ribs.

Halfway across, Wilkie picked up a half brick,

held it out over the missing roof space and let it go. "Let's see how long it takes to drop."

They stopped, waiting. Alan could see the brick plunging past the ruined floors. It went on forever. Then, splash! An awful long way down.

"Blimey," said Tommy. "That's hundreds of feet. And I bet there's another hundred feet of deep water down there."

Alan couldn't help himself. He edged over sideways to have a look. But all he could see was a rippling darkness. Wilkie and Tommy carried on stepping across.

Alan could feel his face going numb and his

insides sliding down like heavy porridge towards his knees. He forced himself to push his feet forward. The parapet felt as if it were swaying like a rope, and around him the world tilted up and down. He wanted to turn back but that was just as far as going forward.

The others had reached the far side and gone through another door. Alan sank down, slid his legs over each side, shuffled his bottom along the stone wall and managed to get over that way. Just as well his friends didn't see him.

He climbed up off the wall, wobbled forward and clung to the doorframe for a moment. He could hear the others talking, their voices low and echoey. Then he heard Wilkie shout: "Down here".

He went through onto another staircase. Somehow, the fire hadn't reached this part of the building. In a corridor, Alan joined the others, his knees still knocking. There were glass panels all along one side, cracked but still whole.

"Must 'ave bin the offices," said Wilkie. Sure enough, there were desks and chairs inside many of the rooms. A lot were smashed and there were papers scattered everywhere.

They picked up some of the sheets but they were just filled with numbers.

"Give me Whitehall 1-2, 1-2. Urgent! We have

found the secret hideout of the Nazi spies," lisped Tommy in a funny accent, holding a broken telephone to his lips, with the listening piece held to his ear.

"We've got the dirty, rotten swine cornered but we are getting short of ammo," cried Alan, waving an automatic chair-leg gun. "Drrrr! Get back you schweinhund," he yelled.

"Get down," shouted Wilkie, as he lobbed a metal weight at the remains of the partition. They ducked behind a desk as the glass splintered into flying fragments.

"We can't hold them off any longer," cried

Tommy into the telephone speaker.

"They'll never get me alive," yelled Alan, getting to his feet and dashing into the corridor, his chair-leg gun at the ready. He sprinted down its length and turned into the sharp right-hand bend.

And straight into a man with a gun.

A real gun.

He's got a gun!

The man lifted the revolver, pointed it at Alan and sighted along its length, eyes focused. Cold. Alan began shaking. He shut his eyes, waiting. Then the click – so loud! Alan waited for the world to explode in pain and blood.

But nothing!

Alan's eyes jerked open. The gun still pointing. Alan staggered, his arms raised. The man didn't even smile.

Then Wilkie and Tommy came rushing around the corner and pulled up, shocked at the sight of Alan, his hands in the air, the man and the revolver. The boys lifted their arms.

The man lowered the weapon and the boys dropped their arms. "Up!" he ordered, and they shot up their arms and watched as he spun the cartridge chamber with a deadly sawing sound. The man peered inside, grunted and jabbed the gun towards them. "Now," he growled, his voice quiet, hard.

He took aim.

Alan heard someone moan – Wilkie. The man paused and studied the boy.

"You!" he ordered. "On yer knees."

Wilkie collapsed with a sob.

A metallic sound, the pistol steady, lowered at Wilkie's head.

Suddenly, the office door behind flung open with a bang. "Ted, I fink we can get an identity card and some ration books for yer," the voice stopped, wavered. "Blimey!"

"Duggie!" cried Wilkie, sniffing back the tears. "Tell 'im!"

"Know these, do yer?" said the man without turning to Duggie, his gun still aimed at Wilkie.

"Yeah, Ted," Duggie's voice shook. "Just kids from round here. Part of me gang. No trouble."

Duggie strode up to Wilkie. "What the hell do you think yer doing?" he demanded, and smacked the boy hard. Alan and Tommy shuffled back, frightened.

"'S all right, Ted," Duggie turned towards him. "Doan need to shoot 'em," he said with a nervous laugh.

Ted lowered the weapon, unsmiling.

"We was just exploring, honest, nuffink else," pleaded Wilkie, pale and scared.

"Who told you we were 'ere then?" demanded Duggie, stepping even closer towards them. Alan and Tommy tried to make themselves thinner, while Wilkie shuffled to his feet.

"Looking for sweets," said Alan. "Thought there might still be some here."

Duggie frowned: "Sweets! What you on abaht?

This was a bleedin' gas mask factory."

"Yeah, but it used to make boiled sweets and that," Wilkie added eagerly. "Me dad said so. He and his mates used to nick 'em years ago."

Duggie shook his head. "Your dad. Always the master criminal." But at least he didn't seem mad anymore. He looked towards Ted. "Shall I bash them?"

Alan literally shivered and he could feel Tommy trembling beside him.

"Nah. Just dump 'em," said Ted, pushing the revolver into his jacket pocket. "Water's deep enough."

"Oh no, please mister…" cried Wilkie. "We don't know nuffin and we won't tell."

Alan saw the black, oily pools waiting and whatever else was swirling down there in their dark depths. He swallowed, his throat tight with dread.

The man stared at them, saying nothing. The long silence was frightening.

"They daren't say anything." Duggie half-pleaded with Ted and half-threatened the boys. "I'll make sure of that."

"You'd better, now get this lot out of me sight." The man turned away and walked back down the corridor.

The boys let out a breath all at the same time

and Alan's right leg kept trembling.

"Who was that!?" exclaimed Wilkie, his voice weak.

"You don't want to know and you don't want to ask," replied Duggie, grimly. "But just so you know, 'is name's Ted Parsons. And he knows how to use that gun. Now come on, shift yourselves before he changes his mind."

They reached the ground floor and stood before the metal door they'd pushed through earlier. Suddenly, Duggie grabbed Wilkie's jacket collar and yanked him close. "You owe me," he growled, close to the boy's face. "I wanna see some good

stuff coming from you. And if not, well, Ted up there won't be pleased."

"Yeah, sure Duggie," Wilkie almost whimpered. "Shall I bring it to yer 'ere?"

"Don't be ruddy stupid," Duggie snapped. "Down the bomb site." And Duggie turned and marched away.

———•———

"That was damn scary," said Tommy when they got well away from the factory. "Good job that gun wasn't loaded."

Alan shuddered at the memory of the click, as the gun's hammer struck home.

"Who d'you think he is, Wilkie?" Tommy asked.

"One of Duggie's contacts with the Mob," pronounced Wilkie, with awe and pride.

"What, like James Cagney?" said Tommy, his eyes gleaming with excitement. "Pah! Pah! Pah! Got yer, yer dirty rat."

"Agghhh!" yelled Wilkie and sank to the ground holding his stomach.

"'S not blinkin' funny," protested Alan. "He weren't pointing the gun at you two and pulling the trigger."

"What was all that with Duggie, just then?" asked Tommy.

Wilkie got to his feet. "Business," he announced.

"You're not still going to nick for him are you?" said Alan in protest.

"Well, 's like he said, it ain't really nicking from bombed houses, now, is it?" Wilkie pointed out. "And anyway, could be some dosh in it."

"Don't they shoot looters, like Alan said?" asked Tommy.

"Now you're being stupid," countered Wilkie. "And don't forget what he said about Ted."

"He don't know where we live," said Tommy, sounding scared.

"No, but Duggie would soon find us," Wilkie pointed out. The smirk had slipped from his face. They stared at each other, the realization sinking in that they were all trapped in a horrible nightmare.

Chapter Seven

Alan and Tommy lay on their spot on top of the footbridge staring along the railway tracks. The barrage balloon swayed at the end of its long steel hawser. Above them, a fighter plane slid throatily across the summery sky. It didn't scare Alan, it was one of ours, a Hurricane. Its sound was… comforting. Not like the nightmare that had gripped him last night.

He'd been in a dark room. He reached out but the blackness was like watery velvet that let his hands slide about uselessly. He daren't move. Anything could be hiding in the room. He thought of crouching on the floor but there might be something crawling about there as well, ready to bite him like a snake.

Then a giant's hand thumped the roof and shook the whole building and Alan could feel his skeleton shaking loose inside his skin. Smash! It slapped the side of the house with a massive crack that almost threw him off his feet. Bang, bang, bang, thumped the giant's fist trying to smash through the bricks and the plaster to get at him. His ears hurt and he ran as a great screaming, tearing sound told him that the giant was reaching towards him.

Down, down he ran, the wooden cellar stairs clopping dully. Above, there were roars and thunder as the angry monster ripped away at the doors and the rooms and the corridors. He reached the dusty floor of the cellar, his bare feet scratching on the coal dust. It was suddenly quiet. And Alan realised he was in even greater danger now for the darkness was creeping towards him ready to wrap itself around him and swallow him into a deep, deep hole of nothingness where no one would ever find him.

Alan yelled in terror and awoke with a shout.

He realised he'd wet the bed.

"You all right, Alan?" asked his mum, popping her head around the bedroom door.

"I had a nightmare and you know…"

"'S aright, dear," she said. "Not your fault. There was no air raid warning and we think they dropped a landmine somewhere near Landor Road. I'll get you a clean sheet."

———•———

"They shipped me bruvver off to Africa," said Tommy. "In 'ancuffs, me dad said."

"He'll be a Desert Rat then," said Alan.

"Yeah. Fink of all that sand. No trees or grass. Nuffink," added Tommy. "Be like the seaside forever."

"They have camels there. And oases. And Bedouins. And they'll be on our side," Alan reassured him. "No one likes the Gerries. They're trying to take over the world and kill everyone."

"Yeah, they're really bad. Can't win, anyway, God's on our side, innee?" said Tommy.

"Well, he has to be 'cos we're the good guys," explained Alan.

"Does He come down and kill the Nazis then?" wondered Tommy.

"No, not really. He doesn't do things like that. Mum says He helps our soldiers shoot straighter than theirs."

"Oh. Yeah, 'cos He's not got a real body or anyfink has he?" nodded Tommy. "Still, He shouldn't let them try and kill us with bombs every night, now should He?"

"Well," Alan pondered, "don't suppose He can be everywhere at once. You know, with so many battles going on."

"What time did Wilkie say we had to meet

him?" asked Tommy.

"Two o'clock. Tasman Road."

"Do we 'ave ter?" protested Tommy.

"Says he's found a place dead easy to get in and get some stuff," said Alan.

"My dad would kill me if I got caught nicking," wailed Tommy.

As Alan and Tommy stared at a two-storey wall, a twisted monument marking what once had been a house, Wilkie announced; "Told you there'd be nuffin to it." He had his mum's old pram beside him. "Been like this forever," he went on. "No one can see us."

"So what we doing 'ere then?" asked Tommy. "There's not even any apple trees to scrump."

"Ah, but I found a secret hiding place," said Wilkie and pushed through a tangle of bushes. They followed him in until they stood in front of a loose barricade of corrugated iron sheets. Wilkie glanced around, heaved on one of the sheets and slid it to one side to reveal an abandoned shed.

"Never guess what's inside," he smirked and pushed open the wooden door.

They followed him inside. It was musty but there were other smells like wood and clothes and the tang of old bicycle oil.

Wilkie clicked on a torch. "There you are then!" he announced proudly.

"Wow!" said Alan and Tommy as the beam panned round and revealed boxes and boxes of stuff: clothes, tins and metal boxes.

"Where's it come from? Must belong to someone," said Alan.

"Nah, 's all right, it's been abandoned," said Wilkie.

"Don't be daft!" protested Tommy. "They wouldn't leave all this behind."

"Straight up," said Wilkie. "Tell it's been here a while. Look at all the dust on them boxes."

"How'd you find this lot then?" asked Alan suspiciously.

"One of the kids down the bombsite mentioned it the other day," explained Wilkie. "Said I'd bash his head in if he mentioned it to anyone else. Anyway, it's probably all nicked stuff."

"Yeah, but who nicked it?" wondered Alan. "They'll be back looking for their stuff, won't they?"

"So what? We won't be here, will we?" retorted

Wilkie. "Now come on, give us a hand, I want ter get some of this stuff over to Duggie before he gets nasty."

He handed them a sack each from inside the pram and began searching through a box. A lot of the tins didn't have any labels on them, so they left them and concentrated on those that had pictures of fruit and vegetables on them.

Wilkie eventually stood and shuffled his sack, feeling the weight. "That should be enough. Old Duggie should be pleased with this lot."

Alan and Tommy did the same with theirs. They looked back at the piles of boxes that still crammed the walls of the shelter.

"We'll come back for the rest later," said Wilkie.

"Fought you said that that was it," protested Tommy. "We're bound to run into the geezers who nicked it in the first place."

"Don't be such a sissy," said Wilkie. "Just be careful's all."

"You know, we could be onto a good thing here," he went on, as he wheeled his mum's pram along the pavement. One of the wheels was a bit shaky and dragged it to the left. He had to keep jerking it back on course.

———•———

Duggie lifted the tins out of the sacks one by one and sniffed. "You been raiding old man Smith's corner shop?" he asked.

He sat on a wooden box in the middle of the bombsite. A small fire still burned even though it was a warm day. A few ragged youngsters threw stones at a bottle nearby. Alan and Tommy waited by the pram parked on the pavement.

"Nah, nuffin like that," protested Wilkie. "Just found it like. And there's plenty more where that lot came from."

"Yeah, likely," sniffed the older boy. "How much?"

Looting

"Couple o' nicker?" ventured Wilkie.

"Five bob," said Duggie. "They've probably gone off."

"Duggie!" whined Wilkie in protest.

"Four bob then," said Duggie, and Wilkie shrugged in defeat.

Later, as Wilkie joined Alan and Tommy, who had waited on the other side of the tip, he opened his fist and showed them the silver coins. "Look at that, three bob. Easy money eh!?"

"Thought you wanted a quid," said Alan.

"Nah, knew he wouldn't go that high. Come on, let's go down the chip shop and get some grub. Then we can divvy up the change," said Wilkie.

Chapter Eight

The all-clear sounded. A hand bell clanged and released the children from the school shelter and they stamped out into the playground ready for the next lessons. The three friends didn't bother going back. It was only English and 'Fatty' Simpson made them copy out the reading book page by page while he did the crossword in his newspaper.

"Let's have another gander down the shed and see what else is there," suggested Wilkie.

"Yeah, but what if they're waiting for us..." Alan began.

"Don't be daft," said Wilkie. "Told yer, it's all scrap that's been left."

Alan and Tommy didn't dare say no.

They crept into the garden, having looked up and down the road just in case. Wilkie hugged the garden wall just before the shelter and waved them down like a platoon commander.

"What's up?" whispered Alan, his voice squeaky.

"Just checking," said Wilkie. "'S alright, it's clear."

A blackbird sang happily on top of a nearby house roof. It couldn't care less what was happening below it, thought Alan. No one could catch it up there, not even a cat.

The shelter looked the same and they pulled away the wooden door. Inside were the boxes full of an assortment of cans. Alan stared at them for a moment.

"Hang on," he said. "I don't remember the baked bean ones being here before."

"'Course they were, you just didn't see 'em," said Wilkie.

"We ain't got any sacks with us," Tommy pointed out. "How we gonna carry the stuff?"

"Oh, just grab a couple of things each," said Wilkie. "Just keep Duggie happy."

They rummaged through the boxes, turning over piles of old shoes, slippers and worn-out clothes. Suddenly Alan spotted a leather case and pulled it clear.

"Wonder what's inside this?"

He opened it with a click. It glowed from the reflected light. "Cor, this must be worth a few bob," Alan pronounced.

"Wow, you lucky bleeder," said Tommy, staring down at the rows of shiny forks, knives and spoons.

"Here, let's have a dekko," said Wilkie, pushing himself close in. "Reckon it's solid silver, that," he announced.

"Blimey," said Alan.

"How much is it worth?" wondered Tommy.

"Hundreds, I reckon," sniffed Wilkie.

"Yeah, but no one would just leave this behind, surely," added Alan, a sense of threat creeping into the shelter and making it go cold.

"Never know, might have been killed in the air raid," said Wilkie reasonably.

"Let's get out of here," said Tommy, with the same sense of urgency as Alan felt.

"Yeah," said Wilkie, picking up on their fears, "Right, good idea, let's get this stuff to Duggie before anyone else gets their mitts on it."

Once outside, Alan felt he could breathe deeply again. Tommy's face looked pale, and even Wilkie was twitching a bit.

"Ready then," he said. "Run!"

And with that he sprinted out of the garden, followed by Alan and Tommy, and straight into the arms of three scowling teenagers, all carrying thick wooden sticks.

"So you're the ones what's been nicking our gear," scowled the ugliest and nastiest-looking of the three. He was years older than them, and as big as Duggie.

"Honest, mate, didn't know it belonged to anyone, just thought it was spare, like," whimpered

Wilkie. His words hung limply between the two groups.

"Dy'ear that, Bartie?" snorted the ugly one. "Claims it was sort of left lying around, like."

The one called Bartie didn't even smile at his leader's witticism. He just growled and slapped his stick heavily into the palm of his hand.

"Gonna hand it in, were yer?" asked the third member of the gang, a scrawny boy with a screechy voice and ears that stuck out wide on either side of his skull.

"You were, weren't yer?" snarled the leader.

"C-course we were, just looking for someone

to give it to," stuttered Wilkie, nodding his head furiously.

Then he carefully placed the leather case of cutlery onto the pavement in front of the leader. He glanced around and gestured urgently at Alan and Tommy, who laid their tins beside the case.

Suddenly, the skinny one and the one called Bartie moved either side of Wilkie. "We ain't got nuffin else, honest!" he cried, his voice breaking with fear.

"You're a real honest one, aincha," declared the leader and thumped Wilkie in the stomach.

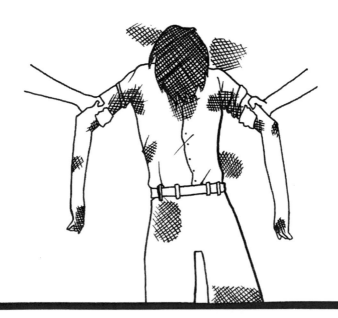

Caught red-handed!

He would have fallen to the ground except the other two gang members grabbed each of his arms.

"Run!" yelled Alan and sprinted. He could hear Tommy gasping and running close behind him. After a while, he realised they weren't being followed. He stopped and looked back and saw, with dread, that Wilkie was being dragged into the garden with the shed they had just looted.

"We couldn't do anything else, could we?" he said, more to himself than to Tommy, who didn't even look at him.

Alan and Tommy walked home in silence along Landor Road, a busy main road that would keep them away from the gang in case they followed them.

"Do you fink they'll torture him to find out who we were working for?"

"Don't be daft," cried Alan, alarmed at the pictures that flashed through his head. "He won't talk," he added, unconvinced.

"But what if he does?" insisted Tommy. "He could tell them where we live and that."

"We could go to Duggie, and he'd beat them up," pronounced Alan.

"I don't want to go near him again," said Tommy. "He scares me."

"Yeah," said Alan.

They sat down on a low wall in Hubert Grove. "Mind, that Duggie might do for Wilkie an' all," observed Tommy.

"And us," added Alan.

"What we gonna do, Alan?"

"I might tell me mum," thought Alan aloud.

"She can't fight Duggie!" scoffed Tommy.

"No, but she could get the cops."

"Yeah, but we've already nicked some stuff and they could arrest us!" protested Tommy. "And if me dad found out, he'd give me a right walloping."

Confused and frightened, they sat in silence trying to think of a way out of it all. And then they heard him, Wilkie, shuffling along towards them from the direction of Tasman Road

They ran towards him. "Wilkie! You all right?" cried Tommy and Alan together.

"Them lousy beggars," cried Wilkie, between gasps of breath, "Kept whacking me and whacking me. And when I told them about Duggie, they said they'd whack him too. And I was to let him know as a warning."

"You didn't tell them where we lived, did you," asked Tommy.

"You!?" cried Wilkie. "What about me!? You ran off and left me to them," he said angrily, sniffing back the tears. "Anyway, Duggie'll sort them out, you'll see."

"I think it's time we stopped this lark," said Alan. "It's getting out of hand."

"Oh yeah, what about me then?" said Wilkie. "I've already had one bashing and I'll get an even bigger one if I tell Duggie we ain't gonna get stuff for him anymore." His gasps had stopped now and he was standing up straight and sounding indignant.

It seemed to Alan that Wilkie hadn't been as badly beaten as he made out, but he wasn't going to say anything.

"We'll just have to find some stuff tomorrow, that's all," said Wilkie and started walking home. "See yer tomorrow."

"Yeah," said Alan. He looked at Tommy and shrugged.

This safety film always scared him. It was bad enough being bombed day and night but bombers dropped other things as well: nasty, silent, deadly things. Bombs that didn't look like bombs. The one shown on the Odeon cinema screen, hanging there from a telephone wire or lying on the pavement, looked like a small harmless tin tube. A toy. Then this kid comes along.

'Cor! Let's see what's inside it,' he shouts to his mate. Alan peered forward, gripping the sides of his seat. 'No!' he mouthed, quietly. And BANG! the kid just disappears inside a black cloud of smoke and fire. Except you never see the sheet of blood or bits of skin and bone that Alan knew would have been flying around all over the place, because he'd seen it, a raw vivid memory of what really happens.

'Remember,' warns the grown-up man's voice, 'if

you see a suspicious-looking object like that one, never, ever, pick it up. It could be a booby trap that can kill or maim.'

Alan nodded in agreement as the lights came up.

"I knew a kid once who found one of them, lying in the kerb," said Tommy beside him. It was a Saturday morning and they'd both walked down to the Astoria for the children's cinema show.

"What happened?" asked Alan.

"Threw a brick at it!"

"Did it blow up?" asked Alan.

"Nah, it was a thermos flask. Smashed it to bits," replied Tommy. "Bloke who'd dropped it was real mad. Chased 'im all up Landor Road."

Then the lights went down again, and the two boys snuggled deep into their seats as the war film blasted onto the screen. This was a proper film, where the good guys killed the bad guys in their hundreds and hundreds. Tommy and Alan thrashed about in their seats, barely keeping their arms from flying about them. All around them, hundreds of other boys and girls twisted and turned as the Spitfires screamed up into the blue skies, spun through deep clouds, their cockpits like flying ragged sheets, swivelled bodily and roared down at the swarm of enemy bombers on their way to blow up people in their houses all over England.

Outside in the sunlit street, Alan and Tommy spread their arms and went full throttle down the pavement, weaving in and out of the massed Nazis, their mouths spitting streams of bullets, tearing enemy fighters to pieces until they exploded in a roaring cloud of flame and burning debris.

At last, they ran out of steam and leaned their backs against a brick wall, heaving and panting. Alan stared up at the soft, white, fluffy clouds suspended in the pale blue sea of the sky. A yearning welled up inside him. It was all so peaceful.

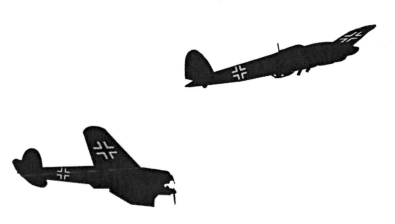

Guilt!

Alan and Tommy slid and crunched their way across the rubble and piles of plaster and wood. A small fire still burned where the back door had once been, that's how recently the bomb had fallen. The explosion had burst open and swallowed the room in flames. One wall remained standing; the rest of the house had tumbled into the kitchen and living room, filling them with dusty red bricks, scraps of wood and muddy water.

"Mum says the firemen always leave a right old mess," commented Alan as they slushed through the deep puddles.

There hadn't been much of a back garden. Nothing but a brick path and two patches of dirt where some stringy looking roses crawled along the ground. The Anderson shelter stood at one end, buried beneath loose soil.

"Do you think they were in there when the bomb came?" asked Tommy, nervously.

"Dunno," shivered Alan, thinking of their shelter back home.

A kitchen chair still sat upright on a section of floor. The table had gone, collapsed in a great whoosh when the floor had disappeared. If you had been sitting on it, would the house have crashed around you, just missing you, or would you have been scraped off the chair and sent screaming down into a roar of bricks and fire? Where had all the people gone who'd sat in that kitchen and had their egg and chips and cups of tea, just like Alan, his sister and mum back home?

"What we looking for?" asked Tommy.

"I dunno," sighed Alan. "Anything to keep Wilkie happy so he can take some stuff to Duggie." He turned over a sheet of plasterboard with his foot.

"Hey Alan, Tommy! 'Ere!" a voice yelled. It

was Wilkie, peering around the wall next to the bombed-out house.

"Don't waste yer time there. You won't find nuffink. Come 'ere."

The house next door looked untouched, apart from long cracks in the brickwork, and some missing window panes with edges of sharp-toothed glass embedded in the frames. Wilkie led them through what was once the front door, which now lay on the hallway floor buried beneath light rubble. "There's no one 'ere at all," he announced, his voice echoing in the emptiness.

"Must be," insisted Alan. It still felt lived in,

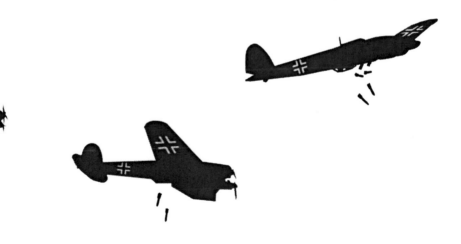

even though the place stank of burnt wood and dampness.

"Nah, been condemned as dangerous," said Wilkie. "They'd have moved them down to that housing shelter in Stockwell. Hey, look at this!" he cried, as he stepped into the door of the next terraced house.

He led them into the front room. Alan coughed because the furniture was black with the choking smell of soggy soot that had whooshed out of the fireplace when the bomb hit next door. Wilkie pointed to a mantel clock over the fireplace. He picked it up and shook it. "It's still ticking, what about that, eh? Bet it's worth a few bob."

He stared at a metal tag at the base of the clock. "To Lance Corporal Reynolds, from the First Company, Royal Fusiliers," he read. He peered closer. "November, 1918. It's an antique this, you know," he said and put it back on the mantelpiece. "I'll get it on me way out. Hey, I bet there's other fings upstairs an' all. Come on Tommy, we'll check around up there, and you have a rummage in here," he told Alan, and led Tommy out of the front room.

Alan heard them clumping up the lino-covered stairs. He stared at the clock. Ten o'clock. Should be on their school milk break by now. Mum would murder him if she knew, but no one seemed to bother at school. He went over to a small book-case. Everything felt slimy with the soot. Alan stared at an old brown photograph in a cheap card-board frame. A young soldier stood to attention, stiff in his uniform with a shy, proud smile on his face. Another photograph was balanced beside it. A young couple this time, the soldier when he was older and the woman with him, his new wife. She coiled against his arm, embarrassed, while he stared down at her like an older brother.

He could hear Wilkie shouting above, eager, looking for treasure like a pirate.

Suddenly, Alan felt he shouldn't be here at all.

It was as if the house was trying to push him out. He had a funny ache in his chest, like when he felt like crying at the pictures. He sighed and put the photo of the young couple back on the mantelpiece. He pushed open the door into the tiny kitchen. That's when he saw the man, sitting in the chair, a mug of tea steaming in front of him. He wore an old khaki army overcoat. Beneath, his legs stretched out in blue-striped pyjama trousers.

The man, who was about the same age as Mr Smiley, the English teacher, looked up at Alan, but his eyes didn't really seem to see him.

"I fought in the last lot, you know. Fought for this country," the man said, spitting his words out in anger.

"Oh," said Alan, not knowing whether to stay or run and yell for the others to scarper.

"Got medals an' all. Didn't get them for pushing a ruddy pen around, you know." Then he held up a row of medals that clinked from a metal bar in his hand.

"Should have shot the lot when we had a chance. Bloody Gerries, always the same, always trying to grab everything. Got nothing, I didn't. Told us it was the war to end all wars. Don't believe nuffin' them beggars in bowler 'ats tell yer."

Then he sighed, his anger fading as he stared

around the kitchen, its walls grubby with the mucky water sprayed from the fire hoses.

"Been here over twenty years. Got this just after we woz married. Ira was always house proud. She wouldn't have liked the mess they made of it. She'd have had me out with the bucket and mop giving it a right scrub. She ain't 'ere anymore, tumour got her."

He sighed again, a long slow puff of air. "Can't be bothered," he added, shaking his head sadly.

A coughing fit grabbed him and he jerked his mug, spilling tea on the floor. Suddenly, his eyes seemed to click into place and he glared at Alan.

"What you bleedin' doing here then?"

"I came in – the door was open an' that." Alan started to say. Then Wilkie burst in behind him, clutching a sheet that clanked and bumped behind him with all the bits and pieces he'd found upstairs.

"Hey, we got loads of stuff," he yelled, and then jammed to a stop when he saw the old man sitting there.

"Blimmin' 'eck!" he shouted.

The man rose to his feet with a roar, tea spilling when he banged it down on the table. He raised both fists in the air and charged towards them. Except his feet got tangled in the chair legs and he had to grab the table to stop himself from falling.

"Run, for Gawd's sake!" cried Wilkie, dropping the sheet and racing for the hallway. Alan almost tripped over the clattering pile of shiny metal plates and books that spilled out from the sheet, but he managed to jump over them and follow Wilkie and Tommy out through the front door.

"I'll bleedin' well kill you when I get my hands on you. Come here, you little devils!" yelled the man from the kitchen.

They didn't stop running for five minutes. When they did, they bent over and heaved with the pain of a stitch, leaning on each other for support.

"An' I forgot the ruddy clock," said Wilkie at last.

"That's it," said Alan, gasping. "No more. I don't care if Duggie kills us, I ain't doing that again. It's not right."

"I didn't know the old man would be there, now did I?" protested Wilkie.

"It was horrible," Alan went on. "Poor bloke's lost his wife, his house and then us lot turn up and start to nick what's left. An' he was an old soldier."

"Yeah," added Tommy. "We shouldn't have been doing it. It's like we're the enemy as well."

"Course we're not like the bloomin' Nazis," argued Wilkie, but his voice was uncertain. "Tell yer what, let's just go for scrap iron next time. OK?"

"Hey, you lot!" said a voice. It was the scruffy boy from the bomb site whom Wilkie had clipped around the ear.

"Oh yeah," said Wilkie, ready to give him another thump for cheek.

The boy backed away, but his face wasn't scared. "Duggie wants to see you lot, nah! At the factory, and he don't want to be kept waiting."

"But..." began Wilkie, but the boy had gone. He looked around at Alan and Tommy. "We're gonna have to go and say..."

"And say what?" Alan asked.

Chapter Nine

They mooched down the road to Brixton High Street, hardly speaking. Wilkie led, his head jutting forward from his neck as though he was forcing himself to face whatever fate awaited them. Alan and Tommy shuffled along behind. Alan looked over towards Tommy. His friend had his head down, staring at the pavement the way you do when you're counting the cracks in the slabs.

"It'll be all right as long as we stick together,"

Alan said, hoping it would cheer his friend up. Tommy didn't even glance at him. Alan called out to Wilkie: "You gotta get us outta this."

Wilkie flicked his eyes back, briefly, and carried on. "It'll be all right, you'll see," he said quickly. "He's probably got a job in mind for us."

Alan stopped and Tommy did too. Wilkie went a few steps ahead till he realised they weren't following him any more. "Well, come on then," Wilkie said. "He'll be waiting for us."

"No more jobs. Wilkie. You've got to tell 'im," said Alan.

"I will, I will," insisted Wilkie.

"Nah yer won't," said Tommy. "You're too scared of him, ain't yer."

"Nahhh!" objected Wilkie, but not very convincingly. "I'll say our parents have found out and are stopping us, like," he ended weakly. "Come on, we gotta get there," he appealed.

Alan shrugged and started walking towards Wilkie. A pause later, Tommy joined him. "Make sure you do, then," he said.

"Yeah," said Wilkie and began marching forward again, looking even more nervous than before.

Then the siren began, winding up and up in waves until it began to shriek its warning over the rooftops. People along both sides of the High

Street stared up and began to hurry off home, or to the nearest public air raid shelter. A bread van revved up noisily and skidded slightly around the corner ignoring the red traffic lights.

The boys stopped. "We'd better get off home," said Alan.

"Too late for that," said Wilkie, "Anyway it's only two more streets and we'll be there. It'll be safe there. I mean, they've already bombed it, ain't they?"

Tommy didn't look too convinced. "What's that got to do with anyfink?" he challenged.

"Well..." began Wilkie, struggling to justify his

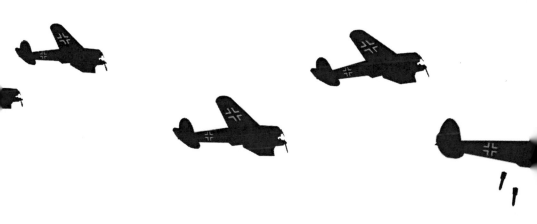

confidence. "Stands to reason, the Gerry looks down through his bombsight, sees the factory wrecked and finks, 'Why waste a bomb on that dump?'"

Alan looked about him. The street was empty now and so quiet. Not a car or lorry in sight. The traffic lights had turned green.

Somewhere distant, a thick, rumbling pulse of sound slowly crept closer. Thump! Thump! Thump! The ack-ack guns were pumping their shells up into the skies. The throbbing grew louder and louder.

"Look at that!" cried Tommy, and they all looked up. Row upon row of black crosses were sliding across the clear, blue sky.

"There's thousands of 'em," said Wilkie. This was a big raid. They stared, fascinated, as a cascade of bombs sparkled earthwards through the air. The boys' eyes followed the slow, dreamy shower down, down, down.

The ripple of bangs and explosions made them jump, especially when one end of a street some distance away flew out in a massive black and grey cloud of bricks and slates. Windows burst into shrieks of glittering glass, spraying across the pavements and into the road.

"Run, flippin' run!" screamed Wilkie and they skeltered around the corner and down the street towards the derelict factory. Pieces of grey slate and smoking, twisting bits of wood fluttered down from the rooftops like a hot, gentle shower.

They reached the broken door of the factory and shoved their way through. Sweat and grime smeared their faces as they leaned panting against the brick walls.

"We made it!" Alan gasped in relief. "I can't believe we're here."

"'Bout ruddy time an' all," came Duggie's voice. He stepped out of the shadows and stood there, staring at them with a hard, unflinching look.

"Blimmin' dangerous out there!" said Wilkie.

"Damn sight more dangerous if you hadn't come," retorted Duggie. "I got a job for yer."

"Yeah but – " started Wilkie.

"No buts," threatened Duggie. "An' it's the last thing I'll want from any of you lot. Yer hardly making me a fortune. I could earn more scrounging around in the dustbins than what you've turned up with." Alan tried not to grin. Duggie was letting them go!

"Give us a chance Duggie, we've only just started," protested Wilkie and then backed away when Duggie jerked his head at him for daring to challenge him.

"Remember my mate?" Duggie continued.

Alan shivered. He could hardly forget Ted, the man with the gun.

"Yeah," said Wilkie, uncertainly.

"He needs your help. To get away, like," continued Duggie.

"But how?" asked Wilkie, puzzled.

"He needs some lookouts," said Duggie. "I got a van coming for him around the back. Need you lot to keep your eyes open while I get him into it."

Ted was leaving! And Duggie didn't want them! So they'd be free, totally free.

"Rozzers," explained Duggie. "Don't want them police creeping up on us."

"Oh," said Wilkie. "Just lookouts, like?"

"That's all. 'Course, be a couple of quid in it."

"What, each?" said Wilkie, his eyes lighting up.

"Don't push it," said Duggie.

"Get on with it." The voice whipped down from the staircase. Alan snapped his head to the voice. Ted.

"Don't worry," said Duggie, suddenly sounding nervous. "It's all sorted. Right you lot," he went on, and pointed to Tommy. "You, tidge up that staircase and get yourself over to that window to keep a shufty on the front.

"And you," he said, pointing at Wilkie, "See that side window? Keep yourself posted there in case

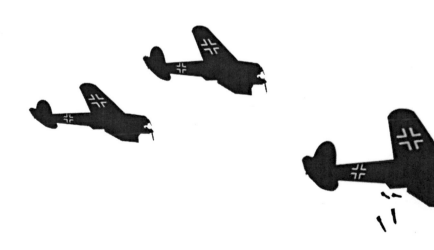

145

they get crafty and try and creep around us."

The boys ran off quickly to take up their posts. Duggie waved to Alan. "You're coming with us," he said. Alan followed Duggie up the iron stairs to Ted.

"How long before the van's here?" Ted demanded.

"Any time. I sent Frank straight away and he should be here in five minutes," answered Duggie promptly.

Ted leaned down and picked up a leather case. It looked heavy. He saw Alan staring at it and lifted it up.

"My getaway fund," he said, like it was a joke, except that he wasn't smiling.

"That was a neat job," said Duggie.

"Pity about the guard," said Ted.

"He shouldn't have been there," Duggie observed. "Trying to be a blinkin' hero." He snorted a sort of laugh.

"He's a dead hero now," said Ted. A quick grin flicked across his face. "Heroes should be in the army, eh?" It horrified Alan. Ted had killed a man in cold blood. He was a murderer!

"Sure, sure," chuckled Duggie, but Alan knew he was just as scared of Ted as he was.

Alan followed them up to the next floor, to the

end of a straight corridor, where a high window, or what was left of it, overlooked the big back yard where lorries had once parked.

"You squat down here," Duggie ordered. "Keep your eyes on that road," he said and pointed to the road beyond the brick perimeter wall. "You see anything, you let out a yell."

"Come on," snapped Ted. They left Alan leaning against the remains of the window and he heard the sounds of their feet clumping down the iron steps. A door banged below.

Alan peered over the edge and saw there was a van there after all, with flaky letters on its side

promising to deliver fresh vegetables, 'Promptly'.

There was a tearing whistle through the air. Then a bomb exploded nearby. A plume of dust and debris rose up, scattering a violent shower of shattered bricks. The cloud made him choke and cough.

The air raid! Odd. He'd forgotten all about it. But his body hadn't. His hands were icy-cold and he could feel a deep shivering welling up in the centre of his chest, shaking him. He stared up through the jagged mosaic of blue sky framed by the broken roof.

He heard the throb of bombers trembling above.

He searched for the planes. Which one would drop the bomb with his name on it, like Mrs Smith had said? Would he hear its scream, streaking towards him? He shook his head. As if it made a difference one way or another. It was like facing the gun as Ted pointed it straight at him. The fear, the waiting, the terrible guessing.

Below, Duggie and Ted hurriedly left the building. They were talking urgently, loudly. Or rather, Ted was jabbing his fist at Duggie who was agreeing as if his life depended on it. Alan craned his head to search over the yard below looking for coppers or soldiers heading their way.

Ted climbed into the passenger seat of the

waiting van, leaned out of the side window and patted Duggie on the shoulder. The vehicle began to draw away slowly.

A hard rod poked Alan in the back of his neck. He stiffened. "Don't say a word," growled a man's voice.

He glanced back and there was a soldier, wearing a red cap and a dark khaki uniform: a military police-man, just like the one who had arrested Tommy's brother. Except this one was armed with a revolver.

"He ain't gonna get far," the man said in Alan's ear. He had removed the pistol from the back of his neck now.

Suddenly the van braked with a screech and

The shoot out

there was a loud crack. A sharp bang answered and the next thing, Ted was out of the van and sprinting back towards the factory.

A soldier appeared in the gateway. Ted, sensing this, turned and fired at him. The soldier cried out and disappeared behind the wall.

"Jesus!" yelled the soldier behind Alan and he rose quickly to his feet. "Stay here and don't move," he barked. And sprinted off.

More shouts, more shots as soldiers and armed, uniformed policemen rushed through the gates.

He could hear yelling from the bottom of the stairs, a pistol shot that bellowed and echoed up

the stair well. Then silence.

Alan let go his breath. He could not stop shaking now and his whole body was frozen.

Suddenly, a voice was shouting: "In here! Quick!"

Alan stumbled to his feet, glanced down at the crowded yard below and ran back the way he had been brought.

He ran into Tommy and Wilkie staring wide-eyed and ashen near the front door. Wilkie was sobbing with fear. "Woss happened?" whispered Tommy hoarsely.

"I think they shot him," said Alan. "You know – Ted, that bloke with the gun."

Voices shouting again. They could hear Duggie's now, pleading: "Don't shoot me, don't shoot."

"Let's get out!" Alan burst out. And with that the three boys pushed through the half-open gate and into the road outside. There was a military jeep parked further along but there was no one with it.

So they ran and they ran and never looked back.

Chapter Ten

They lay across the steel girder above the railway line: Alan, Tommy and Wilkie. They had climbed up there to try and calm down after their frantic escape from the shootings at the derelict factory. No one had said anything for five minutes, each one trying to calm the words spinning around inside his head.

A signal clunked down and a stubby locomotive chugged around the bend, struggling to haul a long

line of trucks. The locomotive hooted once as it disappeared beneath the footbridge, a black cloud of soot and steam rolling back over the trucks.

"We could be put against a wall and shot, you know," said Tommy. Alan and Wilkie whirled round to stare at him.

"Don't be stupid," stuttered Wilkie. "Wha' for? We ain't done nuffin."

"That bloke Ted – he murdered the man in the bank, didn't he!" said Tommy.

Alan nodded glumly.

"And Ted was a deserter," went on Tommy.

"How'd you know that, then?" demanded Wilkie.

"Stands to reason," said Tommy, "They sent in the MPs, just like me bruvver. So the army will shoot him."

"But we ain't deserters," argued Wilkie.

"Yeah, but we did try and help him to escape, didn't we," said Tommy with a triumphant smile on his face. "So there!"

"Nuffin' to bleedin' smile about, you idiot," exploded Wilkie. The boys lay in silence for a few minutes after that outburst. Finally, Wilkie looked across to Alan, who was staring white-faced down the railway tracks. "Reckon he's right?"

Alan shook his head in desperation.

"Yeah, it's all right though," said Tommy, suddenly

sounding cheerful. "They won't know who we are, will they?"

"Cor, maybe yer right," said Alan.

But Wilkie sighed heavily. "Yer forgetting Duggie's going out with my sis. He's bound to tell them where I live."

"Yeah but..." started Tommy, and then went silent. There was no way Wilkie would be able to cover up for them once the police got hold of him.

"We're gonna have to go on the run," said Alan.

"Where to?" demanded Wilkie, "I ain't got no dosh. I might be able to nick a few quid off me dad when he's drunk, but that's about it."

"What about you, Tommy?" asked Alan.

"I got half a crown stashed away," said Tommy. "But I need that for me Christmas presents. Anyway, you got any cash?"

"Nah. Few pennies me mum gave me for washing up," admitted Alan.

"What we gonna do, then?" said Wilkie, his voice trembling.

"We could jump onto one of them wagons and get a ride somewhere. Outta London," said Tommy, enthusiastically. "Yer know, like that film we saw about them hobos in America."

Alan and Wilkie stared ahead of them, recalling the film. "But what we gonna do when we get wherever we get to?" asked Wilkie.

"Catch rabbits and cook them over a fire in a field," said Alan brightening up.

"Yeah!" cried Wilkie. "I'll bring me dad's Army knife so we can kill one and that."

"I'll bring some tea and some tin mugs," said Tommy.

"And I'll nick some matches," added Alan. "When shall we go?"

"Tonight, gotta be tonight," said Wilkie, nodding solemnly.

"We can sneak through the fence in my back garden and wait for a train," suggested Tommy, whose house backed onto the railway.

"What, nine o'clock?" asked Alan.

"Make it ten, then me dad will be passed out in the kitchen," suggested Wilkie.

They jumped off the girder, eager to get on with their plans.

"Better bring a blanket," said Alan. "To sleep in," he added, remembering how the hobos, just like his cowboy heroes, used to bunk down on the ground, wrapped in a single blanket under the stars.

They raced each other down the steps of the footbridge, jumping them two, three at a time.

"See yer later," they cried out to each other.

Except it all turned out worse than they expected.

———•———

When he got home, Alan opened the front door and crept up the stairs to their flat. It was very quiet. Perhaps his mother had gone out visiting friends, or shopping. His sister would have gone with her.

He got to the door and the handle rattled as it always did when he took hold of it. He pushed it open and stopped, his breath whooshing out of his body in shock.

A big policeman stared at him from the kitchen table, a cup of tea in front of him. His large pointed helmet was perched on the tablecloth. Alan's mum sat on the other side, her eyes glinting and blinking as if in pain.

"You must be Alan," the policeman said, his voice deep, almost rumbling. Alan gripped the door handle tightly. He could only nod. He looked desperately at his mum, hoping she would make it all go away. But she just bent her head low, and clapped a hand to her mouth.

"It's all right, Mrs Jenkins, it's all right," the

policeman told her, putting a big hand out to pat her on the elbow.

"I can't believe it. Oh Alan, I can't believe it," his mum burst out, her face red and twisted, staring at him.

"Mum," he cried, but found himself stuck to the floor, unable to go over and tell her it was all right, he hadn't done anything wrong, it was just that everything had happened so fast and there they all were, caught up in something that none of them had ever thought would happen.

159

"Listen, son," went on the policeman. "The others have told us what happened. You couldn't have known."

"You're not going to shoot us?" cried Alan.

The policeman's face seemed to Alan as if it was suddenly gripped in agony, twisting and turning, searching for breath. Then he gave a great big sigh, looked down at his huge shiny boots and paused before speaking again. "No," he said finally. "We've arrested his associates and it will only be a matter of time before we get him as well. He can't get far."

Alan thought about that. "He got away then," he said in alarm. He rushed to his mother, who opened her arms and hugged him tight. "He had a gun, Mum, and he was going to shoot us with it unless we did what we were told."

"There, there, Alan," crooned his mum. "I know you're not a bad boy."

"What I would like to know," said the policeman, "is how you and your friends got involved in the first place."

"Duggie," said Alan. "Wilkie knows him and..." he paused and wondered how much the police knew, "...he promised to take Duggie any scraps we could find..." He tailed off and could see the shed they had plundered and the stuff they had taken to Duggie.

"I'm afraid Duggie was a proper Fagin, Mrs Jenkins, like in Oliver Twist. Got a lot of kids bringing him stuff. Didn't care where or how they got hold of it. We've had our eye on him for some time. That's how we knew about Ted Parsons, the man with the gun."

"He killed a man in a bank, Mum," said Alan staring up at her.

"He died later in hospital, poor devil. Just doing his job, that's all," said the policeman, who now got to his feet.

This is it, thought Alan, his feet and hands going very cold. This is where he arrests me. He stared

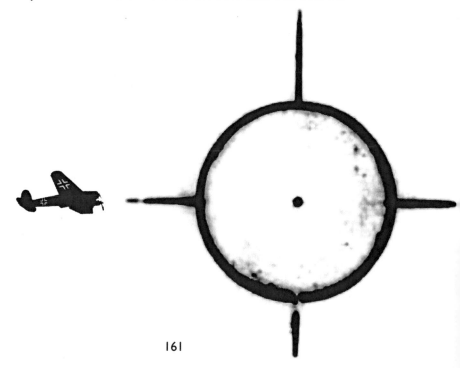

up at the policeman, so big and tall his head almost touched the ceiling.

The policeman put on his helmet and adjusted the strap around his chin. Alan waited in dread for the words to come, words that would tear him away from his mum, his home and everything that was his life.

"But how can it happen?" cried his mum. "How can these kids get so involved in trouble like this?"

"Lot of bad people out there," sighed the policeman. "You'd think with this war on, bombs dropping all over the place, killing innocent people, it'd be enough to worry about. But it's times like this when the rats crawl outta their holes and take advantage. No one's safe from these gangs. And there's plenty of guns about too. As if we haven't got enough bother with Hitler and his evil crew."

"It's living in London, that's the problem," said his mum. "We need to get away."

"You may be right," said the constable. "I'll see myself out," and with that he left the room, quietly closing the door behind him.

Alan stared at the closed door. Astonished. He wasn't being arrested! Now he waited for his mum to speak. Dreading it. But she was silent, looking down at her hands lying in her lap. She looked up at last and stared at him.

"I should have known," she spoke quietly. "I knew something was wrong." She paused and leaned forward to stare into his eyes. Alan could see her eyes tighten and it made him feel very uneasy.

"You've been running wild with those pals of yours for too long and this is where it's got you!" The words hard as bullets, hitting him, hurting him.

"Mum!" the pain in his voice was almost a cry.

"Your school, the teachers – they're no good to you! They're not teaching you anything! You can barely read and can't really write."

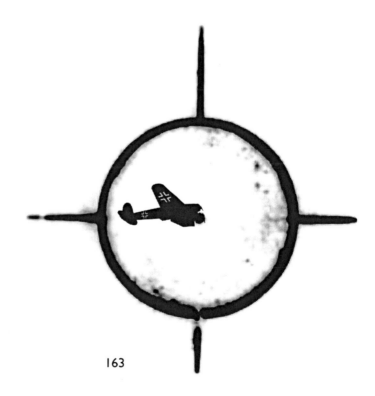

Her head moved close to him. Alan backed away in alarm.

"No more!" She almost hissed the words. "No more. We're going home"

"Home?" asked Alan, confused.

"To Wales!" said his mum, firmly.

———•———

Alan wasn't allowed out for two days and then only if he promised not to see Wilkie. The school had also informed his mum that he wouldn't be allowed back in until the governors had met with staff to decide when it would be appropriate.

She was furious: "Treating you like a criminal, it's not right. It's their fault in the first place, not looking after you."

Alan pretended to be upset. He didn't care; anything to stay off school. He met up with Tommy on the railway bridge.

"My dad went through the roof. He wasn't happy about the cops coming to the house," said Tommy as they spread out in the sunshine across the top girders.

"D'yer know, he even told them to lock me up for me own good!"

"My mum's talking about taking me away," said Alan. "Thinks everyone's got a gun in London."

"Did yer hear that Ted's done a runner?" asked Tommy.

"Still not got him?"

"Nah, he'll be holed up somewhere with his gangster mates."

"Hope he doesn't come looking for us, 'e'd kill us," said Alan, remembering the cold eyes.

"Not with all the cops out looking for 'im!" said Tommy. "Dad's newspaper called him a 'Brutal killer on the run'. Cor! And we were there!"

They sat silently, remembering.

"You seen Wilkie?" asked Alan.

"Did a bunk after 'is dad give him a right bashing," said Tommy.

"I 'eard Duggie's banged up."

They decided to visit the bombsite and have a look-see. It was abandoned.

"Where have all those kids gone?" asked Alan.

"Probably been nicked as well," said Tommy.

"Thought I'd had it when I saw the big rozzer with Mum!" said Alan.

They sat in the burnt-out car and drove it to the seaside and back. Didn't feel the same somehow without Wilkie whooping at the steering wheel.

Suddenly Tommy spotted someone hiding behind a pile of bricks stacked at one end of the site.

"Hey, ain't that Wilkie?" he cried, and waved.

"Not supposed to talk to him," said Alan, as he watched Wilkie sprint towards them, continually glancing over his shoulder as if someone was chasing him.

When he reached the car, he ducked down panting behind the passenger seat.

"Anybody there?" he gasped, his head kept low.

"Nah" said Tommy. "Who's after yer?"

"Yer won't believe it," said Wilkie. "Just seen that bloke, Ted! Yer sure no one's watching?"

"He's s'posed to be miles away, according to the

166

cops," said Alan, glancing nervously behind him.

"Holed up in Tasman Road," insisted Wilkie.

"Yer wot!" cried Alan and Tommy together, scared.

"Hiding out in the house next door to that old shed, yer know," answered Wilkie. "Where we nicked all that stuff."

"Wot, where they beat you up?" asked Tommy.

"That's it," said Wilkie. "'Cept ain't anybody there now. But 'e's got some geezer keeping lookout wiv 'im."

"Did they see you?" asked Alan, looking in the direction of Tasman Road.

"Course not," said Wilkie. "I'd be a dead 'un if he 'ad."

"Yeah!" said Tommy. "Bound to blame us for grassing him up to the cops."

"Wot we gonna do then?" asked Alan, nervously. "He's gonna find out where we live, we're only round the corner."

He pressed himself down beside Wilkie in the passenger seat. Tommy peered over from the driver's seat. "Yeah, what then?"

"Run like the clappers!" pronounced Wilkie.

"Where to?" asked Tommy, a tremble in his voice.

"Gotta tell the cops, before he finds us!" said Alan.

"I dunno..." said Wilkie, worried.

"He's right," said Tommy. "I don't want to get shot."

"S'pose he's got spies out lookin' for us," argued Wilkie.

"Then they're gonna find us pretty soon," said Alan.

"'E's right. Let's go!" shouted Tommy.

"Hang on," said Alan. "Ain't one of us better keep an eye on him, case he does a bunk?"

The two turned to look at him.

"Oh no!" cried Alan. "Not me!"

Chapter Eleven

Alan could smell old clothes and oily bits of car parts as he crept into the shed. Rubbish was piled high up against its walls. There was no sign of the gang who had stashed away the tins of soup and meat. Through a dusty window draped in cobwebs he could see the back door of the house next door.

"All yer gotta do is keep an eye out for him while we tell the cops," Wilkie had said.

"What 'appens if he comes out?" asked Alan.

"Follow 'im."

"Yeah, but 'e might see me," protested Alan.

"Nah 'e won't, Just keep yer 'ead down," said Tommy. "We won't be long. Anyway, I can smell sausages, so 'e's bound to be 'aving 'is dinner."

So Alan was stuck inside the stinky old shed, watching the killer next door.

The back of the house was just a few steps away from him. Most of the windows were broken, the yellow brickwork was cracked, and the drain pipe dribbled dirty stains down the walls.

He jerked back when a shadow blocked out the kitchen window. He waited, then cautiously slid his head forward. He saw the shadow swaying back and forth, and heard the sounds of plates and crockery. He couldn't tell if it was Ted or the other man with him.

The shadow disappeared and there were voices, deep and low. What was he going to do if the men came out? Then he decided they wouldn't. They'd go out by the back door, not the front, and he'd see them in time. Hopefully.

Then clang! Clatter! His elbow had caught some pans hanging from hooks dangling from the shed wall.

He held his breath, waiting. He flicked a look through the window. Nothing.

He stared around him. Nowhere to hide. He had to get out of there.

Voices. One was moving away to the front of the house. "Get the van ready."

It sounded like Ted: harsh and cold.

"Be ready, then," said a voice he didn't recognise. So they had a van. How'd he keep up?

The kitchen door swung open, then banged to. Ted must have gone inside while his mate had come out the back. He must be going round the side of the house to the van at the front, thought Alan. Footsteps crunched away.

Time to sneak out. There was a gap in the hedge

behind the shed. He could edge through it and still keep an eye on what they were up to. Carefully, so carefully, Alan slid open the door and eased through it. The door squeaked only a little. Alan paused.

Silence.

Then he stepped out. Quietly, so quietly, he made his move towards the hedge.

He got to where he could duck down and watch what was going on, hidden by the leaves.

"Gotcher, yer little swine!"

Arms pinned him, hurting. He was violently swung off his feet and spun around. A bony, thin face thrust into his. Spit dribbling, red eyes glaring.

"Who yer got there, Jake?" Ted's voice. Alan could feel his heart banging, his feet scraping on the ground.

"Caught a little spy," answered Jake, and jabbed Alan in the stomach. Alan cried out, tears wetting his cheeks. "Wot should I do with 'im?"

Ted scraped Alan's hair back with a savage tug and studied his face for a moment. "Find out wot he's up to – and then sort 'im out."

Alan couldn't stop shaking. Jake slapped the boy. "'Ear that? Best talk then."

He could smell the man's breath, sour, nearly choking him.

"I, I..." his voice stumbling. Another slap. Now Alan began to cry. Something shiny flashed across his tears. A knife. His face pulled up into it, the man's grubby fist bunched around the handle.

"Sharp, ain't it?" The blade lay cool against his ear, rubbing the flat side. "Before yer lose it, talk. Before I slice off the other one."

"'E's a look out," Ted decided. "But who's he looking out for?"

Ted stared into Alan's eyes.

"Cops," he pronounced. "Finish 'im – and let's get outta here. Pronto."

"Stop right there!" A voice boomed from the

direction of the front of the house.

Jake squealed. "Wot we gonna do, Ted?" His knife waved blindly.

Ted grabbed hold of Alan, jabbing a pistol into his chest.

"Kid's 'ere!" shouted Ted. "So I shouldn't get too close."

Policemen emerged from the overgrown front path, armed, rifles held ready.

"Right, move back," Ted ordered Jake. "Down to the railway line." He pulled Alan along with him.

"Where d'yer think yer going, Ted?" Same booming voice as before. "We're all over the place."

"Not on the tracks yer not," Ted muttered. "Keep moving."

"They got a lotta guns," said Jake nervously.

"Can't use 'em while I got the kid," said Ted. "Nah stop whinin', we'll soon get outta this."

They shoved themselves through the hedge and plunged awkwardly down the short, steep embankment covered in weeds and a tangle of low bushes. Alan stumbled and cried out.

"Shut yer mouf'!" hissed Ted, yanking him viciously by his arm. Alan muffled his pain.

He could hear the police crashing through the bushes above them. "They're gonna catch us!" said Jake, his panic rising.

"Not with trains running on the tracks between us, they won't," said Ted cockily, the gun jabbing the air.

"Wait!" yelled the policeman as he and his colleagues lined up on the top of the banking. Ted spun around with a snarl of rage, wrenching Alan's arm.

Something whooshed past their faces. A rush of sound and wind between them and the policemen forced everyone back. An electric train slapped along the track, its wheels squealing, green carriages rattling, pale faces, one-two-three, blinking down, mouths agape, then gone.

"Let's go," Ted called out, as the train sighed into the distance.

But Jake stood frozen. "I can't. They're gonna shoot me," he cried.

"I will, if you don't," snarled Ted.

"Leave me," Jake pleaded.

"Suit yerself," sneered Ted. He yanked Alan across the bright steel rails. Alan's feet scrambled painfully across the stones between the lines.

Something screamed, high-pitched.

Gone! He's gone ...

The boy looked up. A steam locomotive bore down on them, frantically tooting. It swirled past, hissing and wrapping them in hot, oily, gritty smoke.

Ted stared desperately, counting the shaking, clanking goods trucks speeding past, the constant crash of them numbing Alan's ears. He craned his head to look behind and saw the police following them onto the railway embankment.

Then – woof! Sudden silence.

"Now!" Ted shouted. "It's clear!"

He lunged forward, letting go of Alan's hand in order to steady himself.

A wolfing roar.

Ted disappeared.

Snatched by a terrible suddenness. A whirling blast of hot breath enveloped Alan; he was frozen, rigid.

The passenger coaches twisted by: bang, bang, bang, metal wheels sizzling down the track; grinding, grinding, grinding.

Alan was shaking, stunned.

Arms grabbed him, half carried him back to the embankment.

"What abaht Ted Parsons?" he heard one of the policemen ask.

"Need a bucket fer 'im," said another.

———◦———

Mum had already packed their bags when the police sergeant took him home. She listened to the man in silence, then knelt to Alan and pulled him into her arms and kissed him over and over and over again.

"Look at it this way," the police sergeant said, as he sat sipping tea in the kitchen. "Alan and his mates helped us capture a vicious killer. Though, in the killer's case, it cost him his life. Still," he added, "no loss there."

"Nearly cost my son's life," his mum said, her

voice filled with quiet anger. The sergeant shook his head. "I understand how you must feel," he said. "But, well, he really deserves a medal."

His mum glared. "I don't want a hero for a son. I want an ordinary boy, having a chance to grow up and live a normal, happy life!"

"Called me a flippin' hero!" cried Alan, as he sat on the wall outside Tommy's house with his mates. He'd been allowed to say goodbye for the last time before they caught a train to Wales.

"Yeah!" said Tommy. "They said we should get *medals* for what we did. Dad couldn't believe it, told me I should stop messin' about at school. Medals didn't get you a decent job! But I know me dad, he's beaming alright – says I get my guts from him. He's dead proud of me."

"My dad gave me a clout. For being a snout!" complained Wilkie. "But that's OK too. We did something good, even if it were grassing. That Ted was a right nasty geezer and he would 'ave killed you fer sure, Alan."

The boys all nodded. Whatever price they paid, it was worth it.

"When you off?" asked Tommy.

"Tomorrow," said Alan. "I don't wanna go. But my mum says it'll be great. She's got family there, and I can play outside lots and it's green and full of lambs and stuff."

"Where d' yer say yer were going?"

"Wales," moaned Alan.

"I've 'eard there's dragons there," said Wilkie.

"Yeah!" exclaimed Tommy. "They come down from the mountains and gobble up kids."

Alan stared at his two friends, eyes wide. "Wot!" he protested. "Dragons! I'd be better off staying in London! Even with all the bombs."

They all muttered in agreement. London might be dangerous but it was still home, and besides, all their mates were there.

"Don't care wot me mum says!" promised Alan. "I'm gonna come back soon."

"Yeah," said Tommy. "If she lets yer!"

"Yeah," added Wilkie, "S'long as the dragons don't get yer first!"

Alan stared at him. Then with a whoop and a yell, he flung himself at Wilkie and rolled him to the ground.

"Fight! Fight! Fight!" cried Tommy, and rushed to join in the laughing tumble of bodies.

Afterwards, they lay on their backs panting and staring up at the blue sky, fluffy flakes of cloud sliding across it.

It was so peaceful and still, no rumbling of bombers or screaming of sirens to shatter their happiness.

"Yer know what?" said Tommy. "We're gonna be mates ferever, ain't we."

"Yeah!" said Alan and Wilkie together.

"Ferever!"

THE END

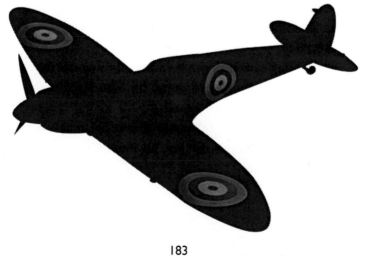

183

Biography of Brian James

Brian James worked for the BBC for over 20 years in both radio and television, producing documentary programmes, such as the South African episode of the highly acclaimed Great Railway Journeys of the World.

As a freelance broadcaster he has worked for both ITV and the BBC and made an American award-winning video documentary for an animal rights campaigning organisation.

His writing career began in radio with one-off short stories and a radio play directed by Alan Ayckbourn. This is his first children's novel.

The photo on the back cover shows Brian as a boy during the war with his dad Jim, his mum Ceinwen and his sister Marlene.